DREAMS AND DESIRE

Penelope's dreams rarely recurred, and even if they did, details changed over time. This particular dream series had never altered until tonight, with this new dream that seemed so real. *Perhaps I should go to Silverthorne castle*, she thought. Curiosity tugged at her, after all. Still, she could not justify the danger Mr. Betterton represented to her on such a flimsy excuse. *Perhaps I should risk it for my family's sake. The last thing they need right now is another mouth to feed.* Penny lay back on the bed and stared into the dark, arguing with herself. Partly she was, she knew, trying to keep herself from falling asleep again, dreading what she might dream next. Each time she had almost talked herself into taking the Silverthornes' position, she remembered James Betterton's handsome face and his wink that was oddly seductive. Her reaction to him was dangerous, she knew. There were more ways to lose her honor than through force. . . .

REGENCY ROMANCE
COMING IN FEBRUARY 2006

The Ruby Ghost

June Calvin

A SIGNET BOOK

SIGNET
Published by New American Library, a division of
Penguin Group (USA) Inc., 375 Hudson Street,
New York, New York 10014, USA
Penguin Group (Canada), 90 Eglinton Avenue East, Suite 700, Toronto,
Ontario M4P 2Y3, Canada (a division of Pearson Penguin Canada Inc.)
Penguin Books Ltd., 80 Strand, London WC2R 0RL, England
Penguin Ireland, 25 St. Stephen's Green, Dublin 2,
Ireland (a division of Penguin Books Ltd.)
Penguin Group (Australia), 250 Camberwell Road, Camberwell, Victoria 3124,
Australia (a division of Pearson Australia Group Pty. Ltd.)
Penguin Books India Pvt. Ltd., 11 Community Centre, Panchsheel Park,
New Delhi - 110 017, India
Penguin Group (NZ), cnr Airborne and Rosedale Roads, Albany,
Auckland 1310, New Zealand (a division of Pearson New Zealand Ltd.)
Penguin Books (South Africa) (Pty.) Ltd., 24 Sturdee Avenue,
Rosebank, Johannesburg 2196, South Africa

Penguin Books Ltd., Registered Offices:
80 Strand, London WC2R 0RL, England

First published by Signet, an imprint of New American Library,
a division of Penguin Group (USA) Inc.

First Printing, January 2006
10 9 8 7 6 5 4 3 2 1

This is my twelfth Regency, and it has been a little more than twelve years since I began reading and writing romances. Reading the genre I once disdained has often saved my sanity in difficult times, as it has done for many of my readers, judging by the letters they send me.

I don't know if this is adieu or merely au revoir, but I am taking a break from writing for a while. In any case, I will still be an avid reader of romance novels, so I dedicate this book to all the writers who enrich life so much for us readers.

June Calvin

Chapter One

*N*ot the dream! Penny tried to escape the snares of sleep, but felt paralyzed as she watched, yet again, the north wall of the castle collapse, carrying with it the people on the battlement. She watched the dust billow up and, when it cleared, searched the void, looking for the woman wearing the ruby necklace. She knew the outcome, of course. There was nothing. Nothing but a gaping hole in the side of the castle. The void almost seemed to suck her into it. She threw her head from side to side, and finally managed to force herself awake, sweating and shaking.

With a sigh Penny threw off her covers. She would not attempt to sleep again, for she knew she might well dream another, even worse, nightmare. They often came in clusters, like the acts in a dreadful play.

She stepped to the window. If it had not been dark, she would only have seen a dingy courtyard. But it was pitch-black, and she yearned for the sight of even that depressing bit of ground.

Drat! I needed a good night's sleep so I would feel my best for the interview today. Her stomach growled, but she ignored it. The half of a roll she had saved from yesterday would be her only meal before her meeting with the Marquess of Silverthorne's secretary at eleven o'clock. She must save it until shortly before she left, to give her energy for the long walk, and to make sure her rebellious stomach would not make the same protest in front of the man who could well determine her fortunes for the next several years. The Marquess had one child, a little boy, and his wife was increasing. If she were hired, she might have employment as a governess for a long time.

A faint light tinged the eastern sky. Penny resolved to use a little stub of candle to draw some more sketches for her children's book. She would blow it out as soon as enough light seeped in through the dingy windows that she did not need it.

James Betterton, knees crossed, swung one booted foot impatiently as he waited in his cousin's elegant townhouse.

"I am plaguey glad this next one is the last. For my ownself, at least. Not for Allison and Thorne's sake, for a less promising lot of governesses I have never seen. Not," he laughed, "that I have seen very many of the species."

Across from him, behind a neat desk, Edward Bartholomew, his cousin's secretary, allowed himself a pinched smile. "Summer is not a good time to find servants. All the ones worth having have either gone with their masters into the country, or gone home to their families for a holiday."

"We should be so lucky, eh, Barty."

"I am always glad to be of service to his lordship."

"Oh, you sanctimonious old goat, you know

you'd rather have some time to visit the museums and coffeehouses. Perhaps pinch a few maids' bottoms."

"Sir!" Bartholomew flushed a brilliant red. He ducked his head to pore over the small stack of applications the Silverthornes had received. "Nevertheless, her ladyship is most anxious to find someone suitable before the second child comes into the world."

James resumed swinging his foot, brushing a speck of lint from the sleeve of his elegantly tailored riding jacket. "Well, I know little enough of who would best suit, but Thorne asked me to assist you, and like you, I must do my duty to my master."

Bartholomew looked up sharply. "Master! He never mastered you, even when you were a youth in his guardianship."

Betterton threw back his head and laughed. "Candor! I admire it, you know. What I love about old family retainers."

Bartholomew flushed again, and mopped his brow with a large handkerchief. "Sorry, sir. Known you since you were in short pants. No excuse to be encroaching, though."

Betterton waved a dismissive hand, and was still chuckling when the butler looked in. "Miss Jones is here."

Bartholomew glanced at the clock on the mantel. "Punctuality. A good sign."

"Hope she doesn't jaw us to death as that last one did. I've plans to go riding after we finish. Ugh. That ugly crone. So full of herself, if we believed the half of it she'd be a candidate for a halo."

"Send Miss Jones in," Bartholomew said to the butler, ignoring the younger man.

Betterton and Bartholomew stood as the young woman entered the room, Bartholomew in the same perfunctory manner as he had greeted the other applicants. Betterton, however, rose to his full height and bowed deeply, confirming the near-sighted Bartholomew's suspicion that this applicant was definitely *not* an ugly crone.

Penelope Jones stood just inside the door, as if poised for flight. "To whom do I give my . . ."

The man behind the desk held out his hand. "I'll take them, miss. I am Mr. Bartholomew, and this is Mr. Betterton, Lord Silverthorne's . . ."

"Cousin. Of course." She actually stepped backward.

James smiled—a smile that did not entirely reach his eyes. *The gorgeous governess! By my stars!* He reached for her references and took them from her resisting hand.

"I'll just hand them to Mr. Bartholomew, shall I?"

"I can't think why *you* are here, sir." She looked at him severely, but had to follow her precious references into the room.

Mr. Bartholomew scowled over his glasses at this impertinence. "His Lordship has asked Mr. Betterton to help me interview the candidates and make a recommendation."

"We are very close," James said, giving her a wolfish grin. She had snubbed him numerous times this season, and his interest in her no doubt had hurt his suit with her employer's two daughters, who might otherwise have joined the throng seeking to be his bride. Not that he had been the only one to attempt to cultivate an acquaintance with the governess as well as the girls she supervised.

Such a pretty companion, though dressed primly and with her tawny hair scraped back in an unrelenting bun at the nape of her neck, could not go unnoticed. Many of the town bucks had tried to entice her into a dance, or approached her as she helped supervise Lady Hartnet's boisterous daughters, hoping to steal a kiss or make an assignation. Miss Jones had snubbed them all.

Penelope uneasily seated herself in the chair across the desk from Mr. Bartholomew, which forced her to sit far too close to the dangerously attractive Mr. Betterton. An uneasy silence fell as the secretary read her résumé before turning to the small sheaf of papers that held her few references. She knew Mr. Betterton was studying her, and felt her color rising.

Ignore him, she told herself. *Your future is at stake here. Don't let a handsome rake distract you.* She sat up straighter and lifted her chin proudly.

"Let's see," Bartholomew murmured. "You attended Mrs. Rawlstone's Select Academy, and subsequently taught there for two years. Then a year later you began acting as companion to Lady Hartnet's daughters, ages seventeen and eighteen. Hmmmm."

The "Hmmmm" was decidedly disapproving. Penelope clenched her hands, bracing herself for the inevitable question.

"What did you do during the missing year, Miss Jones?"

Penelope found it very hard at this moment to follow her father's stern warnings never to lie. She could say she had spent some time with her parents, which was true enough, but it would be a half-truth, of the sort that sometimes came to light at inconvenient times.

James watched in fascination as the various emotions played across Miss Jones's features. She had been most displeased to see him. Her uneasiness was patent at sitting beside him, so near that he could brush her skirt if he swung his boot only a little higher as he restlessly moved his leg across his knee. Did the little flush at her cheekbones indicate any physical awareness of him? He watched her hopefully.

When Bartholomew asked about the missing year, the sudden disappearance of that blush, to be replaced by too-white pallor, caused him to sit forward in his chair, feet placed on the floor, bracing himself as she seemed to be.

"I . . . briefly worked for an employer I may not name. She has written me a reference, but for reasons I would prefer not to explain, she has only signed it 'A lady.' But she was pleased with my care of her daughter."

"Cannot sign it! What kind of reference is that?" Mr. Bartholomew glared at her.

"Allow me to guess," James said. He had thought the minute he laid eyes on her that the young woman was too pretty to be pursuing a career as a governess. "The lady's husband was no gentleman."

She cast him a brief but grateful glance. "Sadly, that is true, in his behavior toward me, at least. He made . . . advances, and when I rejected them, he forbade his wife to write me a reference. But she did anyway, sending it to her friend Lady Hartnet and recommending me to her. In the interim, I had gone to stay with my parents in Wales until I could find further employment."

Mr. Bartholomew was reading her references,

mumbling as he did so. Penelope watched him anxiously, clasping and unclasping her hands.

James took advantage of the interlude to study her further. She was tall, her complexion a smooth, clear ivory. Though she had dressed in colors during the season with Lady Hartnet, she now wore a high-necked black gown of the most severe style. Her hair, a muted gold, was scraped into a bun, but he saw little ringlets trying to escape.

The way she clasped her hands drew his attention to them. The gloves she wore were ancient and splitting at one side seam. Her reticule was large but shabby. James looked again at her gown, and saw unmistakable signs of wear to the fabric.

She really needs this position, he thought, pity welling up in him. *Lady Hartnet must not have paid her very generously.*

Bartholomew looked up at last and shook his head. "I'm afraid you won't suit, Miss Jones."

Her eyes widened. "Wh-why?"

"You have no experience in teaching very young children."

"My youngest students at the academy were six years old," she responded, leaning forward in her chair.

"Yes, but your charge will be a boy of four."

"Four! That is very young indeed to have a governess."

"The boy is precocious. Lady Silverthorne has been teaching him, and enjoying the job tremendously, but she is . . . ah, *enceinte* . . . and won't be able to continue much longer. So"—Bartholomew stood and held out her packet of references—"I wish you the best in your search for employment."

To both men's surprise, Penelope did not immediately take the packet. She laughed dismissively. "I *do* have experience in teaching very young children, in fact. I come from a large family. Elev . . . ten children. My parents taught me and my other older siblings, then turned the younger ones over to us. My youngest brother and sister, twins, began learning their alphabet at my knee, at little more than three. They are precocious, too."

"She has you there, Barty."

Bartholomew looked as if he had just bitten into a rotten egg. "I am afraid it is quite impossible."

"Let me see those references." James snatched them from the desk and read them standing up. "Glowing ones, every one."

"Ah. Yes, well . . ."

"Perhaps you would be so good as to explain why you are trying to reject Miss Jones out of hand?"

Bartholomew mopped at his forehead. "It just seems to me . . . Miss Jones's youth is against her, and . . . do we have to discuss this in front of her, sir?"

"I do not think her youth against her at all, nor her beauty." James gave Penny a wink and a grin. "I certainly think we should forward her information to Lady Silverthorne for consideration."

Penny felt something turn over inside her at the wink. She shot up out of her chair and faced James. "You spend much time with the Silverthornes, sir?"

"Indeed I do. Run quite tame there. Thorne is a combination of brother and father to me, though only a double cousin by birth. And Allison . . . Lady Silverthorne is also my cousin. So you see . . ." His smile faded as she snatched her packet of references from him.

"I thank you for your time, gentleman, but I agree with Mr. Bartholomew that this position is not suitable for me. I shall show myself out."

James realized his mistake instantly. The young woman feared he might try to seduce her. "Now just a moment. This is an insult. You are condemning me on the basis of what that other man did. I would never . . ."

Penny had already started out of the room, ignoring James's protests, when abruptly she staggered and fell back. As he had been following just behind her, James had the not-unwelcome task of catching her in his arms to keep her from falling.

"Wh-what place is that?" she whispered, leaning limply against him while gazing with horror at the painting on the wall next to the door.

"Why, it's Silverthorne castle."

She shook her head. "No. No. I looked up Silverthorne in a guidebook. This is nothing like that picture."

James ventured to shift his hold on her so he could look into her face. Her brief pallor earlier was a positive blush compared to this. "The most common views of the castle are taken from the valley below, from the intact side."

"Oh." She suddenly became aware of the intimacy of their position and pulled away. "Oh. I see."

"Why did the sight of Silverthorne castle alarm you so?"

Penny pressed her right thumb and forefinger to her temples. "It has haunted my dreams since I was a child. Or . . . no, it isn't identical to the one in my dreams, come to think of it." She began to regain some color, and approached the painting. "It is very like, but in my dreams this portion of the battlements is intact."

James stepped in front of her. "That is how it stood until a few years ago. Then the damage done during the civil war and the ravages of time at last pulled down another large section. This picture was drawn by Lady Silverthorne just before repairs were begun."

Penny put her hands over her face and moaned. "It's real. It existed. It all must have happened just as I dreamed it." And for the first time in her life, she fainted.

Chapter Two

*J*ames had known brief fantasies of holding this beautiful girl with the plain name in his arms, but he had never expected them to come true. The result was much less enchanting than the fantasy, for in a dead faint she became a slippery, unwieldy burden.

After a moment or two of struggle, he managed to catch her under the shoulders and knees and carry her to the sofa in front of the fireplace. He laid her down and began chafing her hands and patting her cheeks. Mr. Bartholomew hovered around, making *tsk*ing sounds, until James snapped at him to go find a vinaigrette.

How thin she is! Once again he felt disgust at Lady Hartnet for not adequately compensating her when ending her employment. After all, it was well known that Miss Jones's starchy respectability and good sense had kept at least one of the girls from the grips of an accredited fortune hunter of low character.

Just about the time that Bartholomew returned, ushering before him an anxious maid with a vinaigrette, Miss Jones began to regain consciousness. Her eyelids fluttered open but her eyes didn't immediately focus, allowing James a close, careful look at their unusual color—pale hazel eyes shot through with such a mixture of gold, dark brown, and green flecks that they seemed almost crystalline in structure. When she came to an awareness of where she was and who was leaning over her, his hand on her cheek, the pale hazel eyes seemed made of fractured ice.

Penny sat up abruptly, mortified to find that she had fainted and so placed herself in the hands of this too handsome man with the rakish reputation. Sitting up so abruptly proved hazardous to both of them, however, as this caused her head to bump into his, hard. He reared backward, exclaiming loudly and reaching for his forehead. The bump bounced her back against the arm of the sofa, at which point the maid thrust the pungent vinaigrette beneath her nostrils.

"Stop, oh do stop!" she exclaimed, struggling to get up, hampered by the hovering maid and the fact that Mr. Betterton still sat beside her on the sofa, massaging the bump rising rapidly on his forehead.

"This is most unseemly!" Mr. Bartholomew exclaimed, trying to disentangle the three and only succeeding in further prolonging Penny's inability to rise. At last she simply lay back, her head propped on the curved arm of the sofa, and waited for things to sort themselves out. Her forehead ached abominably; she supposed she must have a bump to match Mr. Betterton's.

The secretary pulled the maid away, Mr. Betterton rose from his place beside her on the sofa, and at last she could attempt to sit up. His hand closed over hers, and Mr. Betterton gave a little tug to assist her. She quickly jerked her hands away and scooted to the far end of the couch, eyeing him nervously.

"Don't look at me that way. Your honor has not been attempted."

She could not resist a smile. "If it was, you certainly do like a great deal of company in your misdeeds!" She instantly repented her words, which could be seen as unseemly, even flirtatious.

That smile, which revealed two hitherto unsuspected dimples deep in her cheeks, did something strange to James's innards. He found himself in the most unusual position of being speechless.

Mr. Bartholomew, however, was far from speechless. He was scolding the maid, loudly disapproving of Miss Jones, and recommending that James remove himself from the room and allow one who knew how to deal with encroaching females to handle the situation.

"Encroaching! The poor girl fainted," the maid protested.

"Out!" Bartholomew ordered her, finger pointing to the door. She scampered away.

"The maid had the right of it," Mr. Betterton growled at the secretary. "You remind me of Agatha Kiesley, always seeing the wrong side of things."

"I don't think so, sir. It is hardly reasonable that she would faint at the mere sight of a painting. This woman is clearly one of those straw damsels seeking to draw you into her web."

"If Miss Jones is spinning such webs, I will go into them quite willingly," James replied, laughing. Penny shrank even further into the sofa, misliking the implication of his humor.

I asked for it, though, with that comment about his misdeeds. What got into me? she scolded herself, primming her mouth.

"But I doubt such is her intention," Betterton went on, subduing his expression. "Do something useful and order tea and some sandwiches. I am downright peckish, and I think some refreshment would do our guest a bit of good, too."

Penelope looked down at her stomach, wondering if it had growled as she lay prone. Certainly the thought of steaming hot tea and nourishment sounded good to it. In fact, the very idea made that too-much-neglected organ rumble ominously. But pride made her rise. Pride and fear at the thought of spending more time with so tempting a miscreant as Mr. Betterton.

"I thank you for the offer, sir, but my business here is concluded. I apologize for inconveniencing you."

"You insulted me, but you did not inconvenience me."

"How did I . . . ? Oh, I beg your pardon. I didn't mean to. It is only that . . . that is, your manner . . ." Mr. Betterton's sideways smile flustered her and did strange things to her thinking. All she knew is that she must get away from here now.

"Where are my references?" she asked, looking around frantically.

"I expect they are scattered on the floor in front of the painting that so alarmed you." Betterton crossed the room in two strides and began gathering them up. She followed him, but before she could even bend down he had them all in hand.

She picked up her reticule and held her hand out for the documents.

"Un-uh. Not until you explain just why that painting distressed you so."

"I did. I have had dreams, bad dreams, about a castle similar to that all my life. But that is nothing to the point. I can't imagine why it caused me to faint. Such is not my nature."

A mixture of fear and hunger, James thought. He withheld the documents. "The price of their return is that you take tea with me and tell me about these dreams. After all, you have aroused a powerful curiosity in me, and I am known to be a very curious man."

"I will avoid the obvious feline cliché. I wish you no ill will, but I really must insist. . . ."

At that moment the maid returned with a tray of sandwiches and seed cakes, and the butler with an imposing tea tray and three cups. Penny's stomach gave another tremendous growl at the sight of the heaped-up food, enough to keep her for days. She felt a gentle pressure in the small of her back, and very much against her better judgment allowed herself to be escorted to the sofa by Mr. James Betterton, who joined her on it and motioned Mr. Bartholomew into a nearby chair. The secretary looked as if he had been sucking on lemons, but sat down, saying nothing.

Penny automatically took over the serving of tea, an art drilled into her by both her stepmother and the headmistress of the academy until she could do it even though half-starved and tingling with dangerous awareness of the man sitting beside her. *Why does he have to have such dark brown eyes? Such long lashes? Such even, white teeth?* As she delivered a cup to Mr. Bartholomew, the secretary looked a little more favorably on her. She took a small sandwich piled high with thinly shaved ham and ate it before attempting to say anything. Neither man spoke, and Mr. Betterton's eager consumption of sandwiches gave credence to his claim to have been hungry.

With him so occupied in eating, she felt emboldened to take a second sandwich, this one a delicious combination of thinly sliced roast beef and watercress on thickly buttered bread. She sipped her tea, and then, seeing that Betterton was starting on his fourth sandwich, she ventured to take one of the seed cakes. She could not help but murmur a little at its delicious flavor and texture.

"Thorne has an excellent cook, no?" James winked at her and took a seed cake himself.

"Thorne? Oh, I collect you refer to the marquess. Yes, quite. I thank you for the refreshments. Please, may I have—"

"Now you know the price you must pay."

Bartholomew began to look alarmed at this incomprehensible exchange.

"Don't swell up, old fellow. I have asked Miss Jones to describe the dreams that caused her distress, that is all."

"In return for what? Really, sir!" Bartholomew said.

"Yes, really. Give me my references," Penny demanded.

James settled back on the sofa, arms crossed. The documents were now lying across his lap. His eyes dared her to snatch them up.

"You are ungallant, sir!"

"I must agree." Bartholomew started to reach for the packet, but stopped at the severe stare he received from his employer's cousin.

"Oh, very well. There are several dreams, though. I hope you are free for a while," Penny said.

"As long as it takes. I had intended to ride with friends but they won't mind if I don't show. If you require hours, we can dine together here." Once again the flirtatious sideways grin sent her nerve ends prickling.

She shook her head and primmed her mouth. "How very glad I am I have already declined to be employed by you."

"By my cousin, that is. In whose house I run tame." He grinned again. "So you repeat the insult. Come, now. The longer you stall, the later you will be in getting home."

She looked with alarm at the window, judging the light. She had a long walk through streets that were barely safe in daytime. Unthinkable to be about at night. The sun still shone brightly, though. Seeing no sign of relenting in her too-attractive tormentor, Penny drew a deep breath.

"Shall I tell them in sequence, or as they came to me?"

"In sequence?"

"Yes. Put together, two of the three comprise a play, almost. A tragic play. I don't always dream them in the right order, and lately a new one has been added which is not—ah, not part of the play."

"Let us have them in sequence, by all means."

She nodded and then looked down, clasping her hands in her lap almost as if in prayer. Did it not occur to this insensitive man that she was distressed, and that telling these dreams would be painful to her? She recalled what Lady Hartnet had said when asking her to discourage her two charges from dancing with Mr. Betterton: "He was quite a rakish fellow until recently, and even today seems more child than man. I believe young girls need a mature man to guide them." She had shrugged off his vast wealth, for wealthy men were the rule in Lady Hartnet's world.

Her ladyship had married a man twenty years her senior, and had apparently enjoyed her recent years of widowhood very much. Her girls had not chosen husbands quite as old as their mother wished, but their fiancés were both in their mid-thirties. Penny judged Mr. Betterton to be not much older than her own twenty-five years, and a good deal younger than her in his care-for-nothing manner. Of course, he did not have to worry about where his next bite would come from, or how to pay the rent for a tiny room.

"Very well, then. In the first dream, I am looking at the backs of two people, the first a tall man in clothing compatible with a supporter of King Charles the first. He carries a blood-soaked sword. He is shoving along in front of him a woman wearing a red velvet cloak. They are in a stone-walled corridor. I have concluded that it is the interior of a castle, based on a later dream. He opens a door and shoves her into a room, slamming the door behind him. It is not a dungeon. There is light coming from three long, narrow windows in the stone walls. There are a bed, a chest, and some other items in the room I can't recall.

"The man says that he has foiled her attempts to avoid their betrothal. 'Your intentions are clear from your attempt to take your jewels with you,' he says as he jerks her around and shakes her. 'My men have recovered a casket of them. But there are more, and you will tell me where they are.'

"Then when she turns toward him, he exclaims and draws back as the hood of her red cape drops back from her head. 'Who the devil are you?'

"She replies to him in Welsh, 'I am Bronwyn, Lady Winifred's maid.'

" 'Speak English!' He slaps her.

"She repeats her response in broken, barely intelligible English. The man then demands to know where Lady Winifred is. She shakes her head. He then threatens to torture her until she does tell. She loosens the fastening on her cloak and lets it drop to the floor, revealing that she is wearing, over a maid's worn clothing, a splendid necklace of rubies and diamonds. She takes this off and holds it toward him and says, again in very bad English, 'Let me go.' "

Both Mr. Betterton and Mr. Bartholomew sat upright and appeared to focus much more intently upon her. Penny worked her fingers back and forth nervously in her lap, wondering why their demeanor had changed. But she needed to finish the tale and be on her way, so she continued her story.

"The man yells, 'Where is she?' She replies, first in Welsh, and then in halting English, that she does not know.

" 'What, were you stealing from her, then? Do you think to buy me off with that? What else do you have on you?'

"He commences searching her roughly, finding nothing else. He snatches the necklace from her hand and puts his fist in her face. 'You will tell me where she is, or wish you had.'

"I won't repeat what he said to her. It is too disgusting. It was many years before I understood the nature of his threats. I'm not sure how much of it the maid understands, but she certainly knows she is being threatened. She begins to cry.

"At that moment, some shouts from above distract him. He puts the necklace inside his doublet and leaves her. She makes no attempt to escape, but instead goes to the cloak and begins ripping at the lining. She retrieves several leather pouches, steps to one of the windows and tries to look out, but she is too short. She pulls a handkerchief from her sleeve and holds it out the window and waves it. Then she throws the pouches out the window, one by one."

Penelope stopped, looking down at her hands.

The two men waited for her to go on, and when she didn't, James prompted her.

"Then what?"

"Then the wall of the room collapses and she begins to fall through the air. It seems as if I am with her, falling, falling, and screaming, until I wake up."

"Good Lord."

At this language, Penny flashed him a disapproving look. "I really must be going."

"No, you really must finish this."

The way he said it, and the intent manner in which both men looked at her, told her their interest in her dreams had changed somehow from curiosity to something more.

She looked anxiously at the window, to see how much light was left. *It must be at least three o'clock now.* It was summer, though. There would be light for several hours.

"The second dream is outside the castle. A castle like the one in your picture, but intact, though obviously battered by cannon. I suppose it is during the civil wars. From this viewpoint I can, in fact, see cannon scattered around me, aimed at the castle across a ravine. Again I am looking at the back of a man and a woman. They stand side by side. The man appears to be a royalist soldier, by his dress and sword. I can make out nothing about the woman, for she wears a shabby cloak with the hood over her head. For a few minutes I think it is the girl from my first dream. The two are watching something happening on the castle battlements, which are intact. Two men are fighting; it looks to be a struggle to the death. To the side stands a woman with long, flowing silver hair."

"She is an impostor," Bartholomew cried, standing up abruptly. "She has read of this or heard of it somewhere. Much of it was tittle-tattle a few years ago."

Penelope stared up at him, and then turned her head to look at Mr. Betterton. Their eyes met. He had a rather hard look on his face.

"Sit down, Barty. Let us not leap to conclusions."

"It is a rig of some sort. It . . ."

"Sit! Down!"

Penelope suddenly realized why both men were looking at her so. "You think the woman on the battlements is your Silver Lady, don't you? Yes, I have heard the stories about her. But this is not your ghost. In my dream she is a living person."

Mr. Betterton nodded. "Please, Miss Jones. I apologize for Mr. Bartholomew's actions. Later, perhaps you will understand them."

She frowned, then shrugged. "Very well. But how you think I could be trying to commit some sort of fraud, when I have done nothing but try to leave you for the last hour, I cannot imagine."

"Tell her to leave. See if she doesn't make some excuse to stay."

"Barty, I would ask *you* to leave, but I expect Miss Jones would not remain *tête-à-tête* with me."

She nodded. She had risen to her feet, and now held out her hands for the papers. Mr. Betterton shook his head.

"I cannot remain. I must walk home. It will be dangerous as twilight falls. You are a careless, heartless bully, sir!"

James glanced at the window. It was quite light. Still, he understood her concern. "You will be provided with a carriage."

"Which could not make it down the narrow streets of Lisle Lane."

Bartholomew sprang to his feet. "Good Lord. The woman comes from Leicester Fields, where brothels abound. Sir, I really must insist . . ."

James abruptly stood and went to the secretary, took hold of the back of his coat, and physically quick-marched him to the door. "Send Mrs. Dickens in, please. She is all that is respectable. Miss Jones need not fear to be alone with me then."

Penny could not see the secretary, but he must have done as he was told. James turned and looked at her, but remained in the door until a woman well past her middle years, plump and motherly, came up to him.

"Mrs. Dickens, will you sit with Miss Jones and listen quietly, please? She is telling me a story I wish to hear without ruining her reputation."

"Very well, sir, but I will do my duty by the child, so you behave yourself!"

Penny's mood eased a little as the redoubtable woman shook her finger in Mr. Betterton's face. She smiled and welcomed her, motioning her to sit down on the sofa. She now had her references, having snatched them up when Mr. Betterton set them aside to deal with Mr. Bartholomew. But the young man's Turkish treatment of his cousin's secretary made her fear to try to leave without finishing what she had begun. She did not know his true temperament, but he seemed not to be a man she would wish to make angry.

Chapter Three

"*N*ow you were saying?" Mr. Betterton said, not the least ruffled by Mrs. Dickens's impertinent behavior.

Penelope ground her teeth at his tenacity. "Where was I?"

"Two men were fighting . . ."

"Oh, yes. Just below them, I saw a white object waving from one of the long windows. Arrow slits, I suppose them to be. The woman watching turns to the man, and as she does, her hood drops back, revealing a richly embroided cap over blond hair. He looks down at her briefly, and I see that his expression, like hers, is one of intense worry. They—we—see the little pouches drop. Then a great rumbling sound begins, and the castle wall begins to disintegrate from below. I see the rocks break loose and come down in great showers. I hear screams. Bodies tumble through the air. Then follows a silence as deafening as the roar of the collapse.

"The man cries out in Welsh, 'Bronwyn! Cariad!' Cariad is a Welsh endearment, which he spoke in a voice of despair. I believe he loved the maid who perished in the collapse of the castle. The woman with him looks at his face and starts to run. He chases her, grabs her by her billowing cloak, and drags her back. He grasps her hair and tugs her head back to expose her neck. In his other hand his sword is raised."

Penelope put her head in her hands.

"Oh, you poor dear, to have witnessed such a disaster." Mrs. Dickens reached over to embrace her. "Where did this happen, Master James? And when? 'Tisna' at Silverthorne?"

"Now, now," he said soothingly. "All of this happened long ago. All over now. She is retelling an account of the collapse of the north wall. I believe it is connected to Silverthorne's most recent ghostly manifestations, of which I am sure you will have heard."

Penny looked up, tears sparkling on her cheeks. "No, I am not. I am telling a dream." She looked wonderingly at him. "I realize your family is a rather superstitious one, but . . ."

Mrs. Dickens primmed her mouth at this implied criticism of her employers. "Dream or not, it is all true. The ghosts have been seen at the castle. Why, the housekeeper at Thorne Hall wrote me—"

"Not now, Mrs. Dickens. Miss Jones has not finished her tale."

"Nor should she. 'Twould make me shudder to hear it, and her to tell it, for he must have cut off that poor woman's head."

Both looked at Penny for confirmation. She shook her head slowly. "I don't know. I always wake up there. It is so awful. As in the other one, I wake up screaming."

"Look at you. Poor little thing, trembling so. I'll have a fresh pot of tea brought, will I? I could do with a cup meself," Mrs. Dickens said.

"By all means. Then hurry back. Miss Jones has yet one more dream to tell," Betterton replied.

"You are as tenacious as a bulldog, sir." Penelope waited in silence until the maid had returned. "This won't take long. Perhaps it will mean something to you, since the others did. In the last dream, which is the one I didn't dream until many years later, when I went to the academy, the maid seems to be addressing me. Of course, she is really talking to the woman in the second dream, you see."

Both looked perplexed, so Penelope elaborated. "In the first dream, the young woman was a maid dressed in a rich scarlet cloak, but underneath it she wore much plainer dress. The woman standing in the trees across the cliff from the castle was wearing a worn old cloak, but her headdress was that of a wealthy woman. It is obvious they had changed places, probably so the mistress could escape her fiancé.

"In the last dream, the maid is bemoaning the fact that she had failed her mistress. By the time I started to have this dream, I had learned a great deal more Welsh, so I understood her clearly. When I first dreamed it, that was all she was doing—pacing back and forth, back and forth, lamenting that her dear mistress's daughter will now be poor and dowerless. She speaks of the necklace, and also of a fortune in jewels. Perhaps that is what she tossed out the window, though it seems unlikely for such small pouches to contain a fortune."

"Perhaps," Mr. Betterton suggested, "she was referring to the casket alluded to by her captor."

Penelope's eyes widened. "I had never thought of that. At any rate, just recently, this dream has changed. The maid looks straight ahead, so that she seems to be looking at and talking to me, but she is urging the 'daughter of Lady Winifred' to hurry up and claim her treasure. Only when it is in the hands of the rightful owner will this maid be able to rest."

"Daughter of Lady Winifred. Hmmmm." Mr. Betterton sat with his elbow on one knee, chin in his hand. "Do you know of any Lady Winifreds?"

Penelope shook her head. "No. I confess I am glad you don't appear to recognize the name. That would have been eerie, to say the least."

"Yes." He stared at her for an alarming amount of time before straightening up. He stood and offered her his hand. She stood up without accepting his assistance, though, which caused a flash of something odd to cross his features.

It seemed to Penelope that she had hurt his feelings. But she doubted he had feelings to hurt. At any rate, she valued her reputation more than any tender feelings by a known rake. *Silly,* she chided herself. *It is not your reputation you fear just now, but what your response to his touch might be.*

"Now may I go?"

"Yes. The carriage is waiting," Betterton said.

She looked at the windows. "I can walk home before dark."

"You are an argumentative woman. You know that, don't you?" His tone of voice was light, and that rakish half smile lit his features. "You will go in the carriage, and I will escort you down the streets it will not pass through."

"I can't allow you to escort me home, sir. My

landlady is most strict, and I am glad that she is. She tries to operate a decent establishment where respectable young women of limited means may live. If I arrive in the company of a well-known . . ." She hesitated, for once guarding her tongue.

"Roisterer? Rake? Villain? Monster? Come, come. Let us have the truth with no bark on it."

"A well-known member of the *ton*." She lifted her chin and stared him down. "That is all. Or any man's escort, for that matter."

"Ah, well-a-day. I shall see you safely home anyway, though at a distance. Don't you agree that that is the correct form, Mrs. Dickens?"

"Indeed I do! And very proper of you to offer, sir. If the young lady wishes, I shall accompany her."

"The very thing."

"It isn't necessary . . ." Penelope stopped her protest when Mr. Betterton held up his hand. "Oh, very well."

To her surprise, a small basket awaited her at the door to the marquess's townhouse. The footman held it out to her, but James took it in hand.

"What . . . ?"

"We have taken up an afternoon of your time. I felt sure you would not accept money in payment, so I asked that a picnic be prepared for you. Now don't protest. You are thin as a rail. I am shocked that Lady Hartnet did not pay you enough to see you through this period of unemployment adequately. At least this will put some roses in your cheeks."

"And fill out that sack of a dress," Mrs. Dickens chimed in, nodding her head vigorously.

"I am most glad it was you who said that and not me." Penny's handsome nemesis grinned, winking at her.

"I cannot let such a calumny stand against Lady Hartnet. She was most generous when we parted. She paid me for six months of work, though I had been in her employ little more than three."

"Then why have you gone from a healthy young woman to a starveling?" Betterton asked.

The genuine concern in Mr. Betterton's eyes made Penelope turn her head and swallow back tears. "I had obligations, you see. My sister is at the academy, following in my footsteps, and my oldest brother is on a scholarship at Cambridge. He is very brilliant and will go far. My family can contribute very little to his keep, and I wanted him to have some new clothes and some money so he won't look contemptible to his classmates."

"Much good you will do them if you starve to death," Mrs. Dickens said. "I don't know what all of those stories were about, but I don't see why they should prevent you from working for the marquess. She is to be hired, isn't she, Mr. Betterton?"

"She has declined the position, Mrs. Dickens. Can you credit it?"

By this time they had been handed into the carriage, and James's eyes crinkled with laughter at the maid's explosion of indignation.

"Not wish to work for the Marquess of Silverthorne? The best master and mistress in all the land. And their babe the sweetest, too. And so smart."

Penelope shrank back from the woman's admonishing finger. "I . . . felt that I had too little practice in teaching very young children, you see."

"Pish tosh. What a foolish girl!" All good nature left Mrs. Dickens. She folded her arms and sat grimly beside Penelope, who looked out the window, pondering bleakly the possibility that the woman was right. She had no other prospects right now, and her savings was near to running out. She had just enough left to take an outside seat on the mail coach to Brecon in Wales so that she could stay with her parents if it came to that, but they had many mouths to feed. How she hated to be a burden to them.

One of the footmen stuck his head in the window and inquired as to her address. She gave him directions to Lisle Lane, which caused Mrs. Dickens to tut-tut once more, and James to shake his head. They rode in silence until they reached Lisle Street, and then the footman handed Penny down. She reluctantly accepted the basket Mr. Betterton handed her, and started off toward the little lane where her boardinghouse stood. A lively whistle began behind her, and she looked back to see Mr. Betterton following her, just as he had promised. She felt a little uneasy. He would know where she lived now. Would he become a problem for her? She thought about stopping somewhere else, but she didn't know anyone in the neighborhood well enough to trust herself to them until Mr. Betterton had left, so she continued on to Mrs. Medley's house and climbed the steps. Mrs. Medley had been watching her approach, as she loved to sit at her parlor window and look out at the life on the street.

"Oh, my dear. I was that worried about you. So late getting home. And I do believe a young man followed you. He looks like the devil personified."

A handsome devil, Penny thought. *And all the more dangerous for that.*

The next morning James apologized to Mr. Bartholomew for his rough treatment of the secretary the night before. He found the other man at his desk, sifting through the morning mail. The secretary accepted the apology graciously.

"It may even be that I gave some provocation," he admitted, much to James's surprise. "I find myself more than curious regarding the young woman's last dream, so I am well paid for interrupting. It is just that I was so sure that she was . . ."

"I know," James said. "And you likely were correct. The street where Miss Jones lives is on the bare edge of respectability." Though he did not say so, he felt sure that at least one of the houses on Lisle Lane was a brothel. *Is Miss Jones the decent, even severely judgmental, woman she seemed, or something else all together? And if so, what is her lay?*

"Sir?"

James started. Had Mr. Bartholomew said something to him as he sat pondering the events of the day before?

"Beg pardon. I was woolgathering."

"Thinking about the attractive young lady. Very understandable. She was an enigma. Whatever her scheme was, though, we managed to foil it, and she will bother us no more. And I have two new applications for governess, so we can move forward."

James nodded and started to rise.

"Sir, won't you tell me the last dream, as a sign

that I am forgiven for my overzealous protective-ness?"

"Oh. Yes, of course." James sat down and told him the gist of Penny's last dream. "I felt sure when she told me the woman in her dream looked directly at her, she would say that she told her the necklace was hers. That was her scheme, I thought. Then she threw me entirely, saying it belonged to 'the daughter of Lady Winifred.' So I am left as curious as you are."

"L-Lady W-W-Winifred?"

"Bartholomew, you have turned pale as a ghost."

With a shaking hand, the secretary fumbled through the pile of mail. "Lord Silverthorne wrote me today, asking me to investigate the history of ownership of all the property within riding distance of the castle. He also wants me to write all noted historians of the civil war period, to find out if any records exist of a Lady Winifred, who possessed a fortune in jewels."

James grabbed the paper from his hands with an oath Miss Jones undoubtedly would have scalded him for uttering.

He summarized the letter as he read out loud, "This ghost wears the ruby necklace Thorne found recently. She walks back and forth in Allison's bed-room all night, speaking in a foreign tongue! She's driving my cousins half-mad with exhaustion. Must find out who the ghost is and what she wants in order to get rid of her. Servants being tripped and vases flying across the room! Thorne thinks lives are in danger." James looked up at the secretary, eyes wide as saucers. "Blast! Miss Jones's dream contains a maid wearing a ruby necklace speaking a foreign language. It is beyond my understanding, but if there is any connection between Miss Jones's dreams and Allison's ghost, we must take action. I'll not let my dear cousin be driven mad by a ghost."

"But what action, sir?"

"Well. Hmmmm. That's a poser. She doesn't like me above half, and you insulted her repeatedly. Not to mention she thinks I am out to seduce her."

"And we think she is out to steal the necklace."

"No, Bartholomew, that can't be it. How could she have known? There is no connection, surely, between Miss Jones and Thorne Hall?"

"One never knows, sir. Servants will talk."

"They certainly find ways to communicate their gossip quickly. But why did she run away like a scalded cat instead of seeking to go to Silverthorne?" James turned around and looked at the painting that had started the whole affair. Allison had painted it as practice during the period she was trying to prepare herself to be a governess, because drawing and watercolors had been one of her less-than-stellar accomplishments.

"Hmmmm. I wonder if Miss Jones, a purpose-trained governess, is a better artist than my cousin?"

Mr. Bartholomew came around the desk and joined him in looking at the painting. "It isn't a bad likeness, sir."

"No, but the perspective is off. Oh, hang it! That is not to the point. If Miss Jones is a qualified governess, she should be able to sketch that necklace. If it is the same one . . ."

"A servant could have described it, sir. Or a worker at the ruins. After all, any number of them saw it when the man's skeleton was discovered with rubies and diamonds draped across its ribs." Bartholomew shuddered at the thought. "I am very glad I was not there that day."

"Surely no one has seen it well enough to describe it clearly."

Bartholomew pondered the question. "No one has seen the ghost, at any rate, but Lady Silverthorne and Marie, her maid."

"That's it! Miss Jones should be able to draw some sort of reasonable likeness of the ghosts, if there is a connection."

"And if there is?"

"Then we shall have to get her to Thorne Hall, one way or another, and see if that ghost will try to communicate with her instead of harassing Allison."

Chapter Four

"*D*raw them?" Penelope examined the sketch pad that Mr. Betterton thrust into her hands, buying time to give her answer. "You want me to draw the people in my dreams?"

"Ten guineas for each sketch. The necklace, the maid, the lady, the soldier."

"Which soldier? There are two armed men in my dream."

"Ummm . . ." James hastily read through Thorne's letter again. "Whichever one is haunting Lady Silverthorne."

"And how would I·know that?" Penelope challenged him.

"Draw both. Fifty guineas, earned honestly. I have brought Mrs. Dickens to chaperon you, and your dragon paces outside."

He referred to her landlady, who had astonished Penelope by inviting her to use the front parlor to entertain her "gentleman caller." Normally those words were preparatory to expulsion from the starchy woman's premises. Penelope supposed it was the presence of the respectable Mrs. Dickens that had convinced her landlady to allow this meeting.

She had been almost as astonished by Mr. Betterton's somber mein as he greeted her, and his continued seriousness as he explained his peculiar request.

"May I know why you would wish such a thing? Because if you think I need charity . . ."

"Not a bit of it. My cousins desperately need your help. A very good woman's life may be at risk, as well as that of the child she carries."

Penny dropped into a chair. She felt the urgency and seriousness of the request. *What am I getting myself into?*

Believing her silence indicated she needed more information, James read to her from the letter.

The female ghost comes into Allison's bedchamber every night and rants and wails in this foreign tongue. If she comes to my bed, the ghost follows. I don't see her, but I hear sounds, very irritating sounds, that make sleep difficult. Allison was already ill with this child. I am very worried about her, especially as several mysterious accidents have occurred to servants around her. Of course, Marie has long since retreated to her cottage, but she warns us that it is the blood-covered soldier who is making the disturbance. She says he is evil, and begs us to be rid of the necklace.

"Why does he not dispose of the necklace, then?" Penelope asked. "Does he value rubies more than his wife?"

James bit his lip to keep from giving this tart-tongued female a scolding. "Not in the least. He has tried putting it in a bank vault in Buxton, and even back into the rubble of the castle, which is where it was originally found, all to no avail. You don't know my cousin Allison, Miss Jones, but she is the kindest, dearest person in the world. That she should be so troubled is distressing enough in itself. But what if the ghost should decide to trip her as it did one of the footmen? He took a nasty fall from the seventh step from the bottom in the front hall. If that had been Allison . . ."

Penelope felt her hand creep to her abdomen, as if she could protect Lady Silverthorne's child by the sympathetic gesture.

"I will do as you ask, of course, although I don't see how this can help. And I won't require payment for it."

Too proud for her own good, James thought. But he wanted her to do the sketches, one way or the other, so he merely handed her the rest of the art supplies he had purchased that morning.

Drawing the portraits of her dream people did not tax Penelope's skills overmuch. She had seen them so often, their features were graven in her mind. Since Mr. Betterton had been so thorough in his purchase of art supplies, she took out the new paints and brushes with great pleasure, and lost herself in turning the drawings into watercolors to better portray her subjects.

The necklace was a little harder. She had only seen it briefly in each dream, and it had seemed but a confection of glittering stones. She teased as much of its features out of her memory as possible, and as she worked on it, she began to feel an almost overwhelming desire to see the one the Silverthornes had recovered from the castle ruins.

She worked until it was dark, perfecting her work

on the necklace after several studies and failed attempts. *It is as near as I can make it without taking out my sketch pad in my dreams,* she thought. Not having the least wish to dream those unpleasant scenes again, she took out a book Lady Hartnet had given her, and lost herself in the guilty pleasure of a romance. This one purported to be by "a lady," and the arch tone and subtle satire of *Pride and Prejudice* amused her until her last candle stub guttered out. *Perhaps I should have let Mr. Betterton pay me,* she thought.

But no. She shied away from that for several reasons, so she turned her thoughts to preparing her few belongings for the journey to Wales. She had run out of money. All that remained was that precious little hoard that would buy her fare home on the mail coach. And an outside seat at that. The very thought made her queasy, but she had no other option. Then she thought of the gowns Lady Hartnet had provided her for the season. *If I sell them tomorrow, I may be able to afford an inside seat.* Cheered by this thought, she hastily undressed and slipped into her bed.

"You must go to Silverthorne castle."

This dream was different, Penelope knew, from any she had ever dreamed before. For one thing, it did not seem as if she were asleep. The maid stood in her room, a slight glow about her lighting the simple furnishings. She had spoken to her, as usual, in Welsh. In her dream, Penelope sat up and responded in that same language.

"What did you say?"

"You must go to Silverthorne castle, daughter of Lady Winifred. The treasure is there, and you must claim it. Please. If you will not do it for your own sake, consider my soul, and that of my beloved Owain."

"Who is the daughter of Lady Winifred?"

"You must go."

Dark. The room was dark, and Penny was sitting in the middle of the bed, the echoes of her own voice in her ear. She had talked in her sleep. It *had* been sleep, hadn't it?

She remembered how her father had explained to her that her dreams were but cobbled together bits of her daily life. Thus, she had started dreaming about the castle after the family visited Brecon Castle near their new home in Wales. He traced her dream of the threatening, mean soldier to an unpleasant encounter with a parishioner of her father's who had objected to paying his tithes. When she had related the collapse of the castle to him, he had thought it referred to her sister Susan's situation. He said it had made her fear that the family itself might fall apart under the strain.

Now I suppose he would tell me that I am dreaming that I should go to Silverthorne Castle because I suspect I should have tried to obtain the governess's position, rather than let Mr. Betterton alarm me into turning it down.

She had never been entirely satisfied with these explanations. She had normal dreams, too, such as her father seemed to think she was describing to him. They rarely recurred, and even if they did, details changed over time. This particular dream series had never altered until tonight, with this new dream that seemed so real. *Perhaps I should go to Silverthorne castle,* she thought. Curiosity tugged at her, after all. Still, she could not justify the danger Mr. Betterton represented to her on such a flimsy excuse. *Perhaps I should risk it for my family's sake. The last thing they need right now is another mouth to feed.* Missing a candle sorely, Penny lay back down on the bed and stared into the dark, arguing with herself. Partly she was, she knew, trying to keep herself from falling asleep again, dreading what she might dream the next time. Each time she had almost talked herself into taking the Silverthornes' position, she remembered James Betterton's handsome face and his wink that was oddly seductive. Her reaction to him was dangerous, she knew. There were more ways to lose her honor than through force.

Penny had packed her belongings and said goodbye to her friends and her landlady by the time Mr. Betterton arrived, looking a little sleepy at the outrageously early hour of ten a.m. She had already given the drawings to Mrs. Medley to hold for him, and stepped out the door just as Mr. Betterton started in, resulting in a near collision.

Confusion reigned for a few minutes, and then he stood, studying her drawings, a frown deepening the grooves between his eyebrows.

"Amazing. You are a very talented artist, Miss Jones."

She could not suppress a smile. "As you have not seen the subjects, you don't know, do you? I might be quite abominable."

Indignation infused his voice. "I hope I am able to recognize good technique. . . . Oh! I collect you are bamming me."

She shook a finger at him. "Language, sir."

The humor in her expression caused him to smile slowly. "You can't resist correcting me, can you?

You should have taken that position with my cousin, for you are a born governess."

That slow, crooked smile did funny things to her insides, and Penny knew she had made the right decision. This man was dangerous to her peace of mind, if nothing else.

"I am not sure how they will aid your cousin, but I hope they may do so. Now if you will excuse me?" She took up her bags again.

"Here, now. Where are you off to?"

Several people were listening, including her landlady, who had opened the door for her in the first place, so Penny could not make the little white lie that sprang to her tongue and tell him she had found a position.

"To Wales, sir, to await prospective employment."

"At least let me take you to the posting house. I have my curricle, so you need not fear compromise."

She should have said no. But she had more than merely her few personal belongings to dispose of. Penny had one carpetbag full of the lovely gowns Lady Hartnet had provided her. The thought of wrestling her bags to the used-clothes vendor a maid had told her about and then walking to the coaching inn made her hesitate. Those bags would begin to weigh a ton before she could complete her rounds.

Taking her lack of a negative for agreement, Mr. Betterton tucked the portfolio under his arms and took her bags from her hand.

"Oh, I left your art supplies with Mrs. Medley."

"I meant for you to have them," he said. "Surely you can use them in your future employment?"

Penny thought longingly of this offer, but shook her head. "They would not fit into my bags."

James reluctantly accepted the supplies, which she had placed back in the large portfolio in which he had brought them the day before. He put them on the floor of the curricle. She explained about the dresses.

"You can leave me at the clothing store, and I will make my way to the inn from there."

"I will take you to the store, and then to the posting inn," he said, mildly but firmly. As he handed Penny up, he mused out loud, "Shame about this. Allison most particularly wanted a governess skilled in art, as she is deficient in that area and feels it keenly."

James felt an urgent need to convince Miss Jones to come to Thorne Hall. He set about the task of coaxing her hither, telling himself it was for his cousin Allison's sake.

"Mrs. Dickens refused to accompany me today, you know." He waited until she turned to him, curiosity in her eyes. "She hasn't forgiven you for rejecting the governess's position. She adores the Silverthornes and cannot comprehend your attitude."

Penny turned her head away, saying nothing.

"It will be lonely for Allison while Thorne is attending to business here and there. She could use some company."

"I thought you would be there most of the time."

"By no means. Oh, I am in and out, but . . ." His eyebrows drew together sharply. "You turned the position down initially because you thought I'd treat you as that previous employer did. Haven't I improved a little in your estimation? No, don't answer that."

She laughed. "Very well. I had rather not."

He skillfully guided the curricle's high-stepping horses through London's busy traffic as he spoke.

"I wouldn't harm you. I wouldn't attempt to seduce you. My father taught me to be a better man than that, and if he hadn't, Thorne would thrash me to within an inch of my life for seducing a decent woman, much less forcing myself on one." He looked at Penny pleadingly. "Come, you clearly need the money, and my cousin needs you."

She considered the sincerity in his voice and features. She remembered the ardent defense of the very respectable Mrs. Dickens. Most of all, she thought of the nearly empty purse in her reticule. As her decision hung in the balance, a voice seemed to speak in her head.

You must go to Silverthorne Castle.

A shiver ran through Penny. *Now I am hearing voices.* Then she heard her own voice responding, "Very well. I will go."

Chapter Five

*A*lmost as soon as the words were out of her
mouth, Penny regretted them. She glanced
over at Mr. Betterton, who was intent on maneu-
vering his curricle through the busy streets. A self-
satisfied smile lit his features, and he lifted his hat
several times to acquaintances. Penny felt her
cheeks burning at the looks she received. Yet those
men surely couldn't think her a "fancy piece," with
her high-necked, plain black gown and her hair in
an uncompromising knot.

With that tilt to his mouth, Mr. Betterton was
very likely imagining dressing her in lavish, low-cut
gowns and parading her in Hyde Park. *Oh, my,
what have I done?* Just as she opened her mouth
to demand he take her to the posting house, he
turned to her.

"Can't wait to introduce you to Lady Silverthorne. Oh, and her mother. A dear creature, and
a parson's daughter like yourself. They'll both be
delighted with you."

This didn't sound like the talk of a man planning
her seduction. Still, suspicion lurked.

"Does Lady Silverthorne's mother live with her?

I thought you said she would be lonely and need a companion."

"She lives in Buckinghamshire, and visits occasionally. She remarried recently, to a country squire who dotes on her. It is quite comical how he refers to her not as Mrs. Whitten, but by her deceased first husband's title, for she was Lady Catherton. Not from pride for having married an aristocrat, either, but out of deep respect. She always refers to herself as Mrs. Whitten but to him she is 'my lady.' "

Penny let her smile echo his, but found herself uneasy with the idea of a woman who so blithely moved up and down the social scale. *I suppose it is easier to move down than up,* she thought.

James wondered why this conversational gambit had caused Miss Jones's expression to change from anxiety to disapproval. Was she about to change her mind? He welcomed the interruption by his friend Sir Beauford Montrose, even though the eager voice calling out to him from a passing carriage probably meant that Beau wanted to borrow money again—a loan that would never be repaid.

Montrose pulled his high-perch phaeton to a halt next to James's just as he turned onto Grosvenor Street. His lovely wife was with him. James tipped his hat to her, rising to bow. She colored up, as she always did at any gentlemanly attentions. Beau's wife was shy.

"My, my. Very fine, James. Very fine. She will pay for dressing, of course, but . . ."

James felt cold fury well up in him when he saw the lascivious look Beau cast upon Penelope Jones. He would have disliked any slur upon her honor in any case, but it could be fatal to his efforts to bring her to Silverthorne.

"Mind your manners, Beau," he said in a tone of steel. "Miss Jones is to be my cousin's new governess. I am escorting her to Thorne Hall."

"An enjoyable duty, I don't doubt."

Lady Montrose had gone pale and still, staring at Penelope intently. Hastening to put her at ease and undo Beau's insinuations, James held on to his temper.

"Duty, Beau. Lady Montrose, may I present Miss Penelope Jones? She, too, is from Wales. Perhaps you have met before?"

Susan Montrose shook her head emphatically, but to James's relief did not snub Penny. "How do you do, Miss Jones?"

Penelope was as pale as Susan, but equally composed. "I am very well, Lady Montrose. And you?"

"Tolerable." She gave a little mock shiver. "It seems chilly for July."

The day seemed fair and likely to be warm, but both Penelope and James quickly agreed to this proposition. Beau waited for the pleasantries to die down. "I say, old man. Haven't got a monkey I could borrow, have you? A bit tight right now."

Five hundred pounds Beau never asked for pocket change. James was in no mood to indulge the man who had insulted his passenger, but to his surprise both women were looking hopefully at him. Lady Montrose he could understand, but what the deuce did Miss Jones care whether he loaned Beau money? Carriages were piling up behind them. "In a bit of a hurry. Call on my man of business," he said, and took out his card case.

Using the tiny pencil inside, he scrawled instructions to his solicitor. "You know the way."

"Oh, that I do, old friend." Beau laughed. "Kind of you. Miss Jones, I do hope you enjoy caring for the Silverthorne brat." He stood up in his carriage, making her an elaborate bow, which James took to be an apology for his previous insinuations. He looked at Penelope, who inclined her head, her expression frosty.

"Must be on our way. We leave for Derbyshire today." James gave his cattle the office to start. They were but five minutes from Thorne's townhouse. Miss Jones was silent, ominously silent, as they completed the trip.

"Here we are. I'll let you off and take my cattle round to the mews, since I didn't take my tiger with me."

Lord Silverthorne's townhouse loomed above them, perfect in its classical proportions.

"I cannot go in there!"

"You aren't going to let Sir Beauford's obnoxious behavior change your plans, are you? He is not a perceptive man, or he would not have behaved so. He soon realized his mistake."

Penelope frowned. Her eyes were on her hands, which were clasping her reticule as if it, and only it, could anchor her to reality.

"I can't go with you to . . . It's near Buxton, isn't it? Travel all that way with you? Even with a maid, what would my reputation be then?"

"Now no changing your mind. Nothing about the Silverthorne's situation has changed, nor has your need for a position." His voice was coaxing, his eyes pleading.

"I know, but . . ." She thought quickly. "I shall go by post."

"Besides, for your information, you will be well chaperoned, and not by a maid, either. You'll be riding in the company of a gentlewoman of unquestioned propriety. Agatha Kiesley is the sister of the previous marquess's second wife, and as respectable as they come. She is also the most disagreeable woman I know. You'll wish you'd made the trip with just a maid by the time you arrive, but your virtue will be unquestioned."

By the time they had reached Buxton, Penny knew beyond a doubt that Mr. Betterton had spoken the truth on at least one point. Agatha Kiesley worked hard every minute to make herself disagreeable. Penny got the impression that she accepted this prospective governess as her traveling companion with an ill grace, but that did not keep the woman from filling her ears with vituperation, concerning everything and everyone along their route. She was equally unsparing regarding their handsome escort. She could not criticize James Betterton enough.

She also had spent hours tearing apart the character of her relation by marriage, the Marquess of Silverthorne. Only two people escaped her censure: the marchioness, her "dear Allison," and Mr. Bartholomew, who accompanied them on their journey.

To this man, who surely must be nearing sixty, she behaved as a flirtatious belle one moment, a solicitous mother or wife the next. Clearly, she was smitten, though at her age, which Penny guessed to be in the mid-fifty's, one might have thought she would have given up any hope of marriage. Her attentions seemed particularly odd considering that Mr. Bartholomew was an employee, a servant of sorts. Given her behavior, which was so high in the instep, one might have thought her the marchioness instead of a pensioner of the marquess, her behavior seemed doubly odd.

Mr. Bartholomew basked in Miss Kiesley's attention and she in his so that Penny ended the journey feeling almost as if *she* were the chaperon, playing gooseberry to two aging, star-crossed lovers kept apart by poverty.

James Betterton rode ahead of them most of the way, only joining them for meals. He had been a model of propriety and more patient under Miss Kiesley's withering fire than Penelope had thought anyone could be. Agatha carped about everything from the sleeping arrangements to the food in each inn along the way. James kept his temper and tried his best to meet her many demands. Only once did he betray that he even took note of the woman's manic temperament.

Agatha had complained about the food arriving late, then said that it was too hot to eat. This observation came at the end of a long list of other complaints, and James meekly agreed with her, but he happened to catch Penny's eye at that moment, and winked at her. She quickly hid her smile in her serviette, and wondered at the fact that it was virtually the only moment Mr. Betterton had seemed to notice her. If he had any rakish designs on her, he certainly hid them well around others.

Her first sight of Silverthorne Castle occurred as the two elderly lovebirds were putting their heads together, whispering. This gave Penelope a chance to get her emotions under control after her first glimpse of those ancient walls. They approached the castle from the undamaged south wall. It loomed from a cliff high above them. A handsome manor lay at the base of the cliff, built late in the last century, in Georgian style.

This view of the castle is the one found in the guidebooks, she thought. *It seems so perfect from here, I could almost doubt that any damage had been done to it.*

"What do you think of it?" Mr. Betterton called to her from outside her carriage window. Agatha promptly leaned over to scold him for giving her a start, but Penelope managed to say, "It is most imposing," which seemed to please him.

"Wait until you see it in the sunset." He grinned down at her, seemingly as proud of the castle as if it were his own. She braced herself for a view of the north face, with its great gaping hole, but the carriage stopped before that came into view.

Servants swarmed out to help the carriage occupants alight and unload their baggage. A tall man who looked enough like James Betterton to be his older brother stepped out onto the front porch, watching as they came up to him.

Penelope expected the marquess, for such she was sure he was, to look less than pleased at receiving Miss Agatha Kiesley. It would be very understandable, if he had any notion of how she felt about him. But he greeted her politely, welcoming her to his home. Then he turned to Penelope.

His expression was ambiguous when he looked at her out of eyes even darker than his cousin's, so dark as to seem almost black. "You are the young woman of whom James wrote."

"I . . ."

"She is. And I have her sketches here. Let us show them to Allison on the instant," James said.

At that moment a woman, obviously increasing, came out the door. "You certainly won't, James Betterton! Our guests must be made comfortable first. There will be time enough later for ghosts and dreams."

Penelope liked her on the instant. Liked her, and pitied her, for she looked like a woman who had not slept in days. Deep circles under her eyes marred her fair skin.

That this was not her usual appearance was demonstrated by Mr. Betterton's cry of dismay.

"Allison! You look half dead!" He clasped her in his arms. "Is this the ghost's doing?"

"Ghosts later." She smiled up at him. "Rest, a chance to change clothes, and one of Chef Pierre's famous dinners, and then we will talk. Come, Miss Jones, Agatha. I will show you to your rooms."

The marchioness had referred to her as a guest, and as a guest she was treated. The room Lady Silverthorne showed her was more luxurious than any she had ever occupied. She wondered what Betterton had written. Had he not explained that she hoped to be a governess? Penny felt she must not impose upon this kindly, frail woman.

"My lady, there is some misunderstanding. I am here to be your governess. At least I hope you may select me for that position. This room . . ."

Allison looked confused for a moment. "You are James's friend?"

"No, I cannot claim that title. We met during the season while I assisted Lady Hartnet in supervising her daughters, that is all. I applied for the position you advertised. I am somewhat bewildered by the notion that my dreams can assist you with your, ah, ghosts."

"Oh. I expect it seems far-fetched to you. But I stand by my selection of rooms. For now you are a guest here. We shall see what the future brings. Jane here will assist you with your unpacking and dressing for dinner."

Lady Silverthorne seemed so near to collapse from exhaustion that Penny could not bring herself to further remonstrance. She smiled and curtsied, and Allison shook her head. "No more of that. I get quite enough curtsies from the staff. I will see you before dinner. We dine early, so join us as soon as you change."

Penny watched her go, and noticed that a stout footman awaited the marchioness by the door. Jane breezed up to her. "That be Strong Ketch. He goes where my lady goes, before her down the stairs and behind her up, in case that there ghost be in a foul mood."

"The ghost is malicious?"

"One of them is. Marie, that used to be my lady's maid, says it is a fierce-looking soldier covered in blood. He plays tricks here and there, tripping people and knocking vases over, that sort of thing. He ha'nt bothered my lady herself so far, but my lord takes no chances with her."

"Very right, too." *Have I landed in bedlam?* Penny could not explain what was going on here, but her inherent disbelief in the spirit world caused her to regard these claims with skepticism.

She turned her attention to unpacking her few belongings and stowing them neatly in the clothes press and dresser. She had ended up bringing the fine gowns her previous employer had purchased for her for the season. The sudden impulse to go to Silverthorne had caused her to forget the plan to sell them, and they had been packed in the carriage along with her other things.

I should have sold them and sent the money to my family, she thought. Yet she had to admit she was glad to have them as the small, energetic maid helped her unpack her things and exclaimed over them. She let herself be dressed quite as if she had a maid all the time, for Lady Hartnet had provided her with a maid for evening parties. Her only jewelry was a cross on a gold chain, which her father had given her upon her sixteenth birthday. She took this from the velvet pouch in which she usually kept it, and held it out to the maid, along with her tortoiseshell hairpins.

Jane showed no disdain as she dressed Penny; rather, she went about the business as if her temporary employer was a highborn lady. She brushed Penny's hair up and collected it at the crown. Taking the pins, she skillfully anchored the bulk that was Penny's heavy hair, and then teased several curls out, using pomade to tame them into ringlets that fell about her face and down the back of her neck.

This is doing it entirely too brown, Penny thought, yet could only smile and praise the maid, who looked eagerly for her approval.

"Now, miss, you do look a treat. And here is Strong Ketch, come back to fetch you down."

"Is Strong Ketch his real name?" Penny could not resist asking as she turned to the hulking man dressed elegantly in the Silverthorne livery.

"No, mum. But he is one of three brothers, and one is called Strong, one Tall, and one Fast. They are all footmen here, and in addition to regular work, each has his special duties, as indicated by his name. Fast, for instance . . .''

The girl let the sentence trail away, for in Penny's doorway, in place of Strong Ketch, stood James Betterton, looking exquisitely handsome in evening clothes.

"I trust I am strong enough to protect you from a nasty ghost," he said, grinning at Penny. "From what I hear, he only gets in a temper when cousin Thorne tries to remove the necklace from the premises, anyway."

Feeling shy for some reason, Penny took Mr. Betterton's arm and they began their walk down the stairs. She was glad of the assistance, ghost or no ghost, for the stairs were numerous.

James looked sideways at his companion and noted her lowered head and neck curved slightly away from him. *Pity she dislikes me so,* he thought. *She is lovely.* He wanted to kiss her, and so forced his mind to other topics.

"My cousin looks quite done in. I certainly hope you can assist her."

Penny frowned and looked briefly sideways at him before returning her attention to the stairs. "I don't see how I can. I have never understood this notion, and feel that I am here under false pretenses, for the room she prepared for me is not that of a governess, I can tell you."

She immediately wished her words had been less waspish, for his expression darkened.

"I don't know if your presence will help or not. Something needs to. She is so altered from when I last saw her."

His concern touched her. *I have been thinking*

entirely too much of myself, and not enough of a fellow creature in trouble, she scolded herself.

He led her into a drawing room decorated exquisitely in the Oriental style. To her surprise, for she had not dawdled at her dressing, her host and hostess, Miss Kiesley, and Mr. Bartholomew were already there, as were four other people she did not know. She was quickly introduced to the marquess's librarian, Mr. Markham Swinton; his estate manager, Mr. William Smith; and the vicar, Mr. Roefield, and his wife.

As soon as she arrived, they went in to dinner. It was indeed as delicious as one would expect from a French chef, and yet not ostentatiously so. The number of dishes were suitable to the number of people present, and there were only two removes in addition to dessert. Penny approved this plan, as she deplored the amount of food normally wasted at the tables of the wealthy, but Miss Kiesley, who sat on the same side of the table, with the vicar between them, could be heard complaining to the vicar that the marquess was as parsimonious as ever.

Mr. Roefield appeared to be quite content, and did not join her in her complaints. Indeed, he gave the woman a rather pointed cold shoulder, instead turning to Penny to ask her about her father's parish. It turned out that they had known each other at school, and his face lit up with joy at learning that her brother John had won a scholarship to Cambridge, and had high hopes of becoming a solicitor.

"A King's Scholar, eh? He does not follow in your father's footsteps, though?"

She shook her head. "He does not wish to be

poor," she laughed. "He is on a walking tour now with several students who will doubtless someday bring him some business. I am sorry to say my brother is hoping to be a successful mushroom."

This brought a laugh from Mr. Betterton, sitting on her other side, and an exclamation of disapprobation from Agatha.

Lady Silverthorne leaned over to asked what had been said and, when she heard it whispered in her ear, smiled at Penny.

"I don't think a hardworking young man who strives to better himself could be considered a mushroom," she said.

"You are entirely too democratic for your own good, and always have been," groused Agatha.

Lady Silverthorne tensed, and looked anxiously at her husband. Lord Silverthorne had not appeared to be listening to their conversation, for at his end of the table he seemed to be in a serious consultation with his estate manager. Penny wondered again if the marquess was aware of Agatha Kiesley's animus against him and, if so, how he felt about it. He had greeted her politely on her arrival. But on hearing the criticism of his wife, his features contorted in a scowl. He opened his mouth, and Penny braced herself for a stinging rebuke from a man who obviously adored his wife.

Apparently Agatha saw his reaction, for she rushed into speech again. "Not that I would criticize you, dearest Allison. You and Thorne have both been so kind to me, taking me in again when my friend could no longer house me. Why, I sang your praises all the way from London, did I not, Miss Jones?"

Penelope sat up straight, mind racing at the di-

lemma she faced. She could not lie, but she hated
to be a talebearer, either. And she heard the des-
peration in the older woman's voice. She pitied
Miss Kiesley, dependent on the charity of a man
whom she despised.

"Indeed, you gave me a very good notion of both
Lord and Lady Silverthorne by your comments,
ma'am," she said.

Chapter Six

*L*ord Silverthorne lifted his glass to Penny. "I have ever admired subtlety," he said. "Here's to one who speaks with exquisite care." She heard Mr. Betterton chuckle quietly, and saw that Lady Silverthorne had relaxed. As for Miss Kiesley, she looked as unaware of Penny's double meaning as she was relieved, and she maintained a chastened silence for the brief space of time that remained of the meal.

"I plan to join the ladies," Lord Silverthorne said, standing. "The rest of you gentlemen may remain here with the port if you wish."

But all seemed aware that something interesting might happen in the drawing room, and men and women filed out of the dining room together.

James gave Penelope a reassuring wink as he took up the portfolio of drawings. "Now for the moment of discovery. Is there a link between Lady Silverthorne's ghost and Miss Jones's dreams?"

"I don't understand why you don't just ask this ghost what it wants," Agatha groused. "You had no trouble understanding the Silver Lady."

"The Silver Lady spoke English," Allison said patiently, seating herself in one corner of a plush sofa and patting the place beside her, inviting Penny to sit there.

Allison's hands shook a little as she opened the portfolio that James handed her and took out a drawing. It was the portrait of the maid.

"Oh! Oh, my!" Allison drew back into the cushions as if to flee a threat. "It is her, to the very life!"

"I knew it!" James was jubilant.

"Are you quite sure, love?" Lord Silverthorne took the drawing from her to study, and she pulled out another.

"See, here is the necklace, very like though not identical to the one we found."

"I could make it more like, now," Penny offered. "I dreamed of the maid again the night before I accepted Mr. Betterton's offer to come here."

"You never told me that," James said.

"I never thought it important."

Mr. Bartholomew and Agatha were tumbling over each other to be the one to insist that the necklace could have been described to her by someone who had seen it. Allison ignored them, taking out the drawing of the soldier.

"All covered in blood, and looking ferocious, just as he does when he throws something across the room," she exclaimed.

"Is that how he looks! No wonder Marie was so frightened of him." Silverthorne took that drawing, too, and handed it to Betterton, who pronounced him an "ugly customer."

"Who is this?" Allison drew out the portrait of the lady. "And this?" She held up the picture of the man who had thrown the maid into the castle room. "Wait. He looks familiar. This is one of the brothers. The murderous one who attacked and killed his brother just before the wall collapsed. Remember, Thorne? I saw that as if in a dream, one night before we found the treasure."

Penny felt as if a great weight pressed her into the sofa. How could this be? How could this woman be seeing ghosts who were the same as the characters in her peculiar dreams?

"Here. Drink this." The deep voice seemed to come from far away. She knew it belonged to Mr. Betterton, and that he was kneeling in front of her, proffering a glass of brandy. The concern on his face warmed her as much as the fiery liquid.

"Are you ill?" Lord Silverthorne leaned over her, and Allison put her hand on top of Penny's, where it gripped the sofa as if she might fall off if she did not hold tight.

"I . . . it just seems so peculiar. How is it possible that you have the same dreams as I?"

Allison shook her head. "These aren't dreams. They are spirits. Perhaps you have been seeing spirits and calling them dreams."

Penny lifted her chin. "Or perhaps you have been dreaming, and calling it spirits."

"Dreams that knock things down and trip people?"

"I just don't believe in ghosts. It is impossible. "

At that moment, the brandy snifter from which Betterton had poured her libation rose from the table and moved sideways, hovering briefly in mid-air before crashing to the stone flagging in front of the fireplace.

Penny saw it all. *What is happening? Things just do not fall that way.*

She put her head in her hands. "Please. I need to think."

"Perhaps the rest of you should leave and let Miss Jones and me compare notes," Lady Silverthorne suggested.

This received many objections, especially from Agatha and Bartholomew, who in different words suggested the same thing—that Penny was an adventuress trying to get her hands on the necklace.

"That is enough! You will wish to retire now. You have had a long day, coming at the end of a long journey." The marquess took Agatha's elbow and began to escort her from the room.

Penny tried to rise and found she lacked the power. Then she felt a strong arm around her waist and Mr. Betterton lifting her up.

"I think that goes for Miss Jones, too. And look at Allison. Burned to a cinder. Let them all retire for rest, and tomorrow they can sort the matter out."

Lord Silverthorne looked ready to object, but Betterton stood firm, and Lady Silverthorne seconded the idea.

"But what if you can't sleep again tonight?" her husband persisted.

"Then I shall continue to take notes."

Penny emerged from her fog of confusion. "Notes?"

"Yes, I have been writing down phonetically what the Ruby Ghost says to me. Mr. Swinton suggested it. He knows several languages." She nodded toward Mr. Swinton, the librarian, once Lord Silverthorne's tutor. "But the ghost is not speaking a language that he recognizes."

"Perhaps I could look at them before I go to bed," Penny offered.

Betterton shook his head. "Tomorrow. Nothing

can or will change tonight. There is too much to be gotten through to cover it all."

Penny's feelings were mixed. She was grateful for his concern, for it was on her behalf he acted. But she was also frustrated, because she wished to satisfy her curiosity.

Allison held out her hands to her husband, who assisted her to her feet. "I believe you are right, James. We are all exhausted. We have plenty of time. Tomorrow, then?"

After the women retired, Thorne saw the vicar and his wife out, and then asked to speak to James privately in his study. The other men went their separate ways.

"You seem to take a protective interest in our young guest," Thorne observed, pouring them both some brandy.

"She needs protection, poor thing. Half starved when she came to us seeking work. And yet refusing to work for you because . . ."

"Refusing?"

James felt his face flush. "Yes, she feared I might seek to force myself on her, or seduce her."

"Whatever gave her that notion?" Thorne scowled at his cousin.

"Don't become the censorious guardian to me again, Thorne."

"Sorry. I apologize. Glad those days are over."

James relaxed his suddenly guarded stance. "It was nothing I did. Or at least, not lately. Oh, I asked her to dance with me during the season, but she refused with frosty reserve. I think her employer, Lady Hartnet, told her things about me, harking back to the days when I was raking about town with Jared and that rackety group. Add to that, she was forced from her first position because her charge's father made advances, which she repulsed rather firmly. Gun-shy now."

"I did not know. I haven't seen any qualifications or references on her. I confess I'd like to know more about her. I'd damn sure like to know what she is doing with this Ruby Ghost dancing around in her head."

"Ruby Ghost? Allison used that term, too."

"That is what Marie calls her, because of the red cape she wears and her stunning ruby-and-diamond necklace. Would you like to see it?"

James eagerly nodded his assent, so Thorne took him into the library and opened a wall safe. He brought out a wooden box and set it on the desk. When he opened the lid, the opulent collar of rubies and diamonds set in gold filigree chains seemed to light up the room.

"Whew! That is something. I wonder what it is worth?"

"Several thousand, I shouldn't doubt, merely for the stones. And the fact that it is an old piece might add value. I know that Allison likes the design, though she could never wear it."

"Why not? You could have it repaired."

"Pick it up."

James reached for the necklace. The instant his hand touched it, a cold chill struck him, painfully freezing him from fingers to elbow. He dropped the glowing jewelry instantly.

"Phew! That's strange. Is it cursed?"

"I don't know. I had hoped I was done forever with these manifestations of the unseen world. Don't really believe in curses, but then . . ."

"You didn't believe in ghosts until the Silver Lady led you to our treasure."

"Just so. I wonder if Miss Jones could handle it without discomfort."

"I almost wish I hadn't sent her on to bed. But she was quite done in. Riding in that carriage with Aunt Agatha and Bartholomew must have been exhausting. Clever the way she avoided exposing Agatha, while conveying to you the true nature of her comments about you."

Thorne smiled. "Yes. Neat turn of phrase. Well, if she's able to take this thing away from here and rid us of these ghosts, I'll gladly give it to her."

"It'll be a fortune to her. And she'll likely give all of it to her relatives. Apparently has a plethora of siblings and is very fond of them."

"That does her no harm in my eyes."

"Nor mine. Yet I could wish she'd do something for herself."

"Careful. You're in a fair way to being love-struck."

"Wouldn't mind if I were. Almost three years since I've had the funds from the treasure. Meant to marry and settle down. But it's not as easy as it seems. Women tumbling all over themselves to attach me, of course, but I don't want that kind of marriage. Mean to say, I'd like to have a relationship like yours and Allison's. But it won't be with Miss Penelope Jones."

"Why not? She isn't *ton*, but she is obviously gentry, well-spoken and intelligent. She'd never disgrace you in a drawing room. I realize marrying beneath one's class requires caution, though."

"Oh, it's not that. It's her. She doesn't like me, not by half." James sighed. "I thought if I behaved with the utmost propriety on our trip from London, she'd see I wasn't a monster, and warm up to me. But she grew even cooler as the trip went on. She's so straitlaced, I'm probably as well off to have her give me the cold shoulder. But I can't help wish it were otherwise. You always said I'd regret the way I behaved, back in my wild days. And you were right."

The maid was waiting for Penny when she returned to her luxurious bedroom. Her clothes were put in the press, her few personal possessions arranged on the dresser. The bed was turned down, and never had a bed looked so inviting to Penny. She allowed herself to be undressed, smiling a little at the attentiveness of the eager maid.

Does she know I am just a governess? she wondered. Too tired to ponder even the events of the evening, much less the future, she headed for the bed. *I could sleep on a granite slab,* she thought as she eased herself between the covers of the most comfortable bed she had ever occupied.

She feared she would dream, here in this strange place where her dreams had become Lady Silverthorne's ghosts, but she didn't. She fell asleep immediately, and was utterly amazed to see that light poured into the room when she awoke.

What had awakened her, apparently, was the maid peeking into the room to see if she was up yet. Jane apologized and started to leave, but Penny beckoned her in.

"I do not usually sleep so late. What time does the family break their fast?"

"That's just it, miss. Lady Silverthorne sent me here to ask you to join her in her sitting room."

Penny dressed quickly, directed the maid in arranging her hair in a simple braid knotted at the nape of her neck, and hurried along to the marchioness's room. To her relief, Lady Silverthorne's appearance had altered very much for the better. The deep circles under her eyes were gone, and her expression was animated.

"There you are! I hope you slept as well as I did. You deserve to have, for I doubt not I have you to thank for an uninterrupted night's sleep. It did worry me to think our ghost might have turned her attentions to you."

"No, ma'am. I slept soundly through the night."

She seated herself at the small table, where Allison presided over both a teapot and a coffeepot, and accepted a cup of tea. Seconds later, a footman brought in a tray laden with covered dishes, steaming hot. Penny chose eggs and kippers, as well as toast, which she slathered with butter and jam. *How good it is to be able to eat to satiety.*

I shall have to take care, or I'll put on flesh, she thought. But she put aside such caution this morning. *My clothes still have quite a bit of room for growth.*

To her surprise, the marchioness did not initiate a conversation about the ghost and her dreams. She accepted this decision and they discussed the weather and the Silverthorne's precocious son. Penny shared a few memories of her active younger siblings' antics, and they laughed as easily as old friends, so much so that Lady Silverthorne quickly suggested they use first names.

"Oh." Penny frowned a little. "I don't know about that, ma'am. I still hope I might be considered as your governess, you know."

"Just when we are private, then?"

Penny nodded, wondering if they would often be private. Yet the talk flowed so readily between them, she could easily see this woman as a friend rather than an employer.

When they had finished their morning meal, Allison took Penny up to meet her son, Jason. As they climbed the steps, Allison said, "I thought we'd save the subject of your dreams and my ghosts for when Thorne and Jamie could join us. That way you won't have to tell everything over and over."

Penny nodded her assent. "I doubt not your husband thinks me a want-wit, the way I collapsed in a heap last night."

"Nothing of the sort. This is all quite extraordinary. Add to it to the exhaustion you would naturally feel after your journey, and I expect you were as tired as I was."

Jason, Lord Riggswheel, was a merry, demanding little creature who had clearly had a great deal of maternal attention and expected more. He was eager to begin his lessons, too, which astonished Penny.

"He can read," she murmured as the boy bent over *Mary and Her Cat*, which had already been colored and handled until it was near to falling apart.

"He started picking out words almost a year ago, whenever I read to him," Allison said. "So I started him on his alphabet and now I am constantly seeking things he can read that are at his level and yet not depressing. They are not easy to find. In their eagerness to teach morals and manners, most writers of children's literature end up writing things that could give their young readers nightmares!"

"I know what you mean. My father often complained about how depressing and even frightening children's literature is. It is all very well to teach them lessons as they read, but too much vivid moralizing can frighten them."

"What do you think is the solution?"

Penny considered telling her about the books she had written, but decided it might be a bit forward on such little notice. Besides, most of them were with her father in Wales.

"There is a bookshop in London, not in the fashionable part of town, but in Skinner Street, where the owners publish books for children that are quite well done. It is called the Juvenile Library." She did not mention that the proprietor was the infamous Godwin, anarchist, atheist, and father of the scandalous though talented Mary Wollstonecraft Shelley. She did not know the Silverthornes' political views, but few members of the aristocracy found Godwin's views tolerable.

"I shall send off for their inventory as soon as possible."

"Mama, Mama, what's this word?" Jason took his mother's chin in his hand and redirected her attention to him.

"Dreadfully spoiled, I fear. This is one reason I wished to find a governess before the new babe arrives."

Penny smiled hopefully. If Lady Silverthorne would hire her, and if the expected second child was a girl, she might have employment for many years. She watched mother and child together and felt a little pang around her heart, realizing she likely would never have a child of her own to tuck so close to her side.

"Mama, what does *bachgen* mean? And *cariad*?"

Allison shook her head. "I don't know. I don't think they mean anything." She looked at his book, seeking vainly for those words on the page.

"Yes, they do. That pale lady with the pretty necklace says them to me."

Allison jumped so hard the book fell out of her hand. "What pale lady?"

"The one who visits every morning. She says those words to me over and over. I like her, but I wish she wasn't so pale. Is she sick?"

Allison looked at Penny, stark terror in her eyes.

Chapter Seven

*J*ason looked up at his mother questioningly. Penny took his hand, drawing his attention away from Allison's frightened face. "*Cariad* is an endearment in Welsh. It means 'dear' or 'darling.' So is *bachgen*, which would be as if I were to call you a darling boy."

"It means she likes me, then. I knew she did, for she comes here when I wake up before Nurse, and sings to me. I don't know the words, but it is a pretty song."

"Is . . . is there anyone else with her?" Allison asked.

"No, Mama. Should there be?"

Allison shook her head and hugged her child to her. "Nurse will take you for a walk in the garden this morning. Miss Jones and I have some business to take care of."

Jason wasn't best pleased with this, but did not cry as they left. On the stairs, Allison clasped Penny's hand tightly, for the footman who had gone with them earlier had apparently thought she would be in the nursery longer, and was nowhere to be seen.

"We must get to the bottom of this," Allison

exclaimed, and Penny agreed, though she wondered how. Such things were entirely beyond her ken. "I hope Thorne and James are back from surveying the progress on the repairs to the castle."

They were. The four were joined by Mr. Bartholomew, who was there to take notes. Penny once again told her dreams, omitting no small detail. By the time she had finished, Lord and Lady Silverthorne appeared to be utterly convinced that she had dreamed of the time when part of their castle collapsed, killing several of their ancestors.

"We have to find out what these ghosts want. The Silver Lady and her knight lingered waiting to pass the treasure on to us three," Allison said. "The Ruby Ghost and her bloody soldier likewise must have something holding them here, bound to earth."

It is very unbiblical, Penny thought. She could just imagine her father's reaction to all of this. Still, she wanted to help the distressed mother. "Perhaps I should take a look at your notes."

Allison nodded. "Thorne has them."

Lord Silverthorne handed Penny the pages of neat handwriting, which seemed to contain gibberish. She frowned over the mess for a while, then began to sound out what Allison had written.

"Yes. That is it," Allison said. "Or very close."

"This first part is clear, then. It says, 'My lady, this necklace and treasure are not yours. They must be given to the daughter of Lady Winifred."

"Yes, I thought she said Lady Winifred. Then she begins to pace back and forth, wringing her hands and crying as she says the next part."

Penny spoke the sounds aloud several times, shaking her head in puzzlement. "It seems to be a lamentation about something she—the maid—did wrong. No, that is a plural pronoun, I am guessing. *They* did something that cost this Lady Winifred her fortune. Something about a daughter, too. Hmmm. There was mention of a daughter in my last dream."

She looked up, trying to envision in her mind's eye the two dreams that told what had happened.

"The maid tried to exchange the necklace for her freedom, but surely she understood that a man so ruthless would not be satisfied with that. And then she tipped those parcels out the window and waved her kerchief in signal. And the lady was standing across the way, watching, with the soldier. Oh! How I wish I could talk to this sprit directly, the way you can. And why did the soldier attack the lady when the castle collapsed? It wasn't her fault."

James looked at Thorne. "Haven't you started inquiries, trying to find something out about this woman?"

"Yes, but with just a first name, it will be like looking for a needle in a haystack."

"The next thing you know, that poseur will be claiming she is related to your ghost so she can claim the necklace."

All four turned, startled, to find that Aunt Agatha stood inside the door.

"How long have you been standing there?"

"I came in just after you did. I felt insulted that no one took note of me. I meant to wait until you did, so—"

"So you could enjoy giving us another scold," Thorne said.

"Thorne, never mind. Aunt Agatha has said something very important. She may just have given us the solution." Allison turned to Penny. "Could it be that you are, in fact, descended from one of these women?"

Penny looked from face to face, interested to see the emotions there, from curiosity on Allison's and her husband's, to concern on James's, to suspicion on Mr. Bartholomew's. She didn't have to look at Agatha to know how she felt, for she began to screech, "That is just what she wishes you to think."

"I very much doubt it. My mother kept a very detailed genealogy of our family. My father showed it to me after her death. He said it would be mine someday. There are no Welsh ties until my father. I am assuming this lady was Welsh, to have a maid who spoke only that language."

She ransacked her memory. "There were no ladies at all, in fact, until the mid-1750s when there was a baronet on mother's side named Sir James Iltry. Father said mother was enormously proud of that connection. He used to twit her on her fascination with genealogy, given that her pedigree was as pedestrian as his, containing mostly respectable gentry of little fortune or fame."

"Iltry." The marquess snapped his finger. "That might be very helpful. There is an estate near here by that name. Perhaps a perusal of the Iltry family tree will shed some light on matters. I'll put Mr. Swinton on the case right away."

"That's crown land now, isn't it?" James looked questioningly at his cousin.

"No, it is trust land, held in abeyance until the heir or heiress is made clear. I currently hold the lease, so there should be no problem gaining access to the family records."

Penny felt very odd all of a sudden. "Heiress?"

"I don't perfectly recall the details, but I believe the estate was to be passed on in its entirety to a single heir. There being multiple heirs with equally valid claims to it, it was placed in trust."

"How long has this gone on?"

"Oh, fifty years or so, I think. Complicated mess. I know because I tried to buy it once. Land marches with mine near the castle."

A dead silence fell over the room, as several adults held their breath at the same time. Allison was the first to speak what they were all thinking. "Perhaps it is connected somehow to this whole thing. Perhaps Penelope Jones is the heiress."

"That would be unlikely. If she were the last survivor, or even one of a competing few, she would surely be aware of it. More importantly, the very fact that she has several siblings means that even if the claimants were limited to her own family, and none of them had children, only the last survivor could inherit it. It doesn't go to the eldest. It goes to the only."

Penny put her head in her hands and her shoulders shook.

"Are you laughing or crying?" James asked, coming to bend over her in concern.

"A little of both. I am my mother's only surviving child. She died when I was about four. My siblings are all half brothers and sisters by my father and stepmother. But surely there must be several other branches, for the heir to be unknown. If I were in any sort of close contest, surely I would know of the possibility of such an inheritance."

"Stranger things have happened than that a family lose track of an inheritance. Even titles have gone unclaimed." Thorne strode toward the door. "I am going to set Swinton to work right now."

"While you are at it, why don't you bring the necklace for Miss Jones to look at?" his wife suggested. He waved assent as he strode out the door.

While he was gone, Allison rose and went to Agatha, who had taken a chair across from her sofa. She whispered into the woman's ear, and a sour look and a red flush indicated that Agatha did not like what was said, but she nodded her head in assent.

Penny tried to shut them all out: James with his dark eyes dancing with good-humored curiosity; Allison with her thoughtful, kind countenance; and the two unfriendly faces of the secretary and Agatha. She looked down at her hands, knotted in her lap, and tried to think what her father had told her, so many years ago, about her mother's family genealogy. *I will write him,* she thought. *I will see if he knows anything of a possible inheritance.* In fact, she resolved to set this whole situation before her father in detail. He would be skeptical, of course, given that he did not believe in ghosts. But he would be fascinated, she was sure. How would he explain a connection between her dreams and Lady Silverthorne's? Even if he was right in saying, as she knew he would, that Lady Silverthorne's "ghosts" were in fact dreams, how would he explain that they both dreamed of the same persons?

So lost in thought was Penny that she was unaware that Lord Silverthorne had returned to the room until suddenly a box moved into her field of vision. She looked up at him as he opened it, then back down, drawing in a deep breath as she saw the necklace that had so long been a part of her dreams, real and glowing, in front of her.

"Would you like to pick it up? You can see it better spread out."

She nodded mutely, and picked up the elaborate jewelry. She lifted it into the air and turned it this way and that, *tch*ing a little over a broken area with some missing stones.

"A shame it isn't intact," she murmured. "It is so beautiful."

Something about the way Lord and Lady Silverthorne and Mr. Betterton were looking at her made her feel peculiar.

"What? I didn't mean to criticize it. It is only . . ."

"It doesn't bother you to touch it?" Mr. Betterton's lively brown eyes were wide with amazement.

"No, of course not. I mean . . . oh, you mean because it is associated with so much death. Yes, in that sense, of course." She started to put it back in the box, feeling she had somehow injured the family's sensibilities.

"No, that was not my cousin's meanings," Lord Silverthorne said, laughing. "You have no peculiar sensations? It is not unpleasant to hold?"

She shook her head, mystified.

"Why should it be unpleasant to hold?" Agatha snapped. "It is just metal and stones. Here, I'd like to see this marvel." She snagged the necklace from the box. It had not been in her hands more than ten seconds when she suddenly let out a yelp and threw it across the room.

"That thing is possessed! Fetch the vicar. He should perform an exorcism. If you ask me, you should throw the accursed thing into the grave with that skeleton and let that be an end to it."

"That's already been tried," Thorne said solemnly. "The ghosts only increased their persecutions." He picked up the necklace and hastily returned it to Penny.

"I don't understand. What sensation did you feel when you touched it, Miss Kiesley?"

"Cold. Bone-deep cold, all the way up to my elbow." She massaged the offended joint as she spoke.

"Is it the same for you?" She turned to Allison.

"Yes. For all of us. At least . . . James?"

"Felt as if I'd plunged my arm into a snowbank and left it thirty minutes."

Penny shook her head, lifting the necklace again as if to test its temperature. "It simply feels like a necklace to me. But I wonder if Miss Kiesley doesn't have the right of it. It sounds like some sort of possession." She put the jewelry back in the box, a moue of distaste quirking her mouth. "I plan to write my father for guidance on this. Have you discussed the matter with Mr. Roefield, Lord Silverthorne?"

"The vicar does not believe anything has been seen, heard, or felt. He explains all as dreams and delusions. Very convenient, for that way he doesn't have to deal with the ramifications."

Penny smiled. "I think my father might have reacted similarly. But once he learns that Lady Silverthorne and I have such similar dreams or . . . experiences, perhaps he will respond more substantively."

"Get a Catholic priest in here," Agatha demanded. "Lose no time about it. The old church may have some odd notions, but it knows how to deal with these situations."

Allison shook her head. "I don't believe there is any demonic possession. What I think is that the Ruby Ghost wants the same thing our Silver Lady wanted—to return a family heirloom to the rightful owner. And I think we are in train to do just that." She cast a minatory eye at Miss Kiesley, who had already opened her mouth to protest. "Now, Aunt Agatha, remember what I said to you!"

Miss Kiesley opened and closed her mouth several times.

"That seems premature to me, Lady Silverthorne." Penny shook her head vigorously. "In spite of Miss Kiesley's and Mr. Bartholomew's suspicions, I am not seeking to gain possession of this necklace."

"I know you are not." Allison leaned over and clasped her hand. "But you won't refuse it if it will help me sleep and . . . and protect my dear Jason, will you?"

"Jason!" Lord Silverthorne leapt to his feet.

"Yes, Jason. The Ruby Ghost has appeared to him."

"Though with no hostile intent," Penny hastened to put in. "She calls him her darling in Welsh, and sings to him."

"By Zeus," Mr. Betterton exclaimed. "She'd better have no hostile intent. Do that child a harm, and I will personally grind that bauble up into powder and throw it in the river!"

Chapter Eight

*P*enny had just time enough to marvel at the ferocity of the young man she had thought of as easygoing, before a noise startled everyone in the room. She turned toward the sound of the loud bang, which was followed by clanging and clashing of metal against metal, and then against stone. The bare spaces on the wall told what had fallen: a large metal shield that had hung above two massive swords. The swords, too, had deserted their post to fall to the flagging surrounding the large old-fashioned fireplace.

Miss Kiesley began shrieking and couldn't stop, even though Mr. Bartholomew tried his best to comfort her. Lady Silverthorne had plunged into her husband's arms, and Penelope felt the urge to do the same with Mr. Betterton, who stood openmouthed, surveying the damage.

Ultimately Allison had to go to Agatha and shake her to restore silence to the room.

"Sorry," Mr. Betterton muttered. "Guess our ghosts took exception to that."

"Very likely," Lord Silverthorne said dryly. "Though I do appreciate your protective instincts toward my son."

"Love him like my own," Betterton said. "What's to do, Thorne?"

Silverthorne shook his head. "At a guess, I'd say not to hint at destruction of that necklace."

Allison glared at him. "You are remarkably calm about this."

"Panic will gain us nothing. Oh, do stop sniveling, Agatha. Bartholomew, take her to the front drawing room and get her some brandy, will you?"

"Miss Jones looks as if she could use a touch of that medicine. Wouldn't say no to it myself," Betterton said. He approached the heap of ancient armament. "Fairly banged up."

"Would you like some brandy, Allison?" Thorne looked at his wife briefly, then turned fully toward her. "Dearest, are you ill?"

"I . . . I'm feeling a bit faint. Nerves, I suppose. I think I'll go upstairs and rest. After I check on Jason."

"I'll check on Jason," Mr. Betterton said.

"Wait!" Penny called out, panicked, as it looked as if she would be left holding the necklace. "This needs to be put back in your safe."

"Yes, of course, for the moment. James!" Lord Silverthorne called out to his cousin, who was already racing up the stairway. "Come put this necklace in the safe. I'll check on Jason."

James passed Lord and Lady Silverthorne on the stairways as he came back down. Penny stood at the bottom, the necklace held out as if it might bite her.

"Don't blame you for being wary of that thing."

She shook her head. "More wary of being accused of stealing it.

"You aren't afraid it is cursed?"

"I am not of a superstitious nature, sir." Her rapidly beating heart gave the lie to her bravado.

"I suppose you will say no ghost brought down that armament."

"I will say I think it highly unlikely. It has hung there forever, judging by the outline on the wall."

He looked closely at her. "So it is just a coincidence. Just happened to come down when I threatened to destroy the necklace."

"Yes. Or at least . . . it certainly could be." Her racing heart gave the lie to her calm reply.

"Hmmmm. Well, let's not take any chance. You bring the thing along, will you?"

He led her into Thorne's study, and opened the wall safe. Penny pointedly turned her back on him as he did so.

"Punctilious sort, aren't you?"

"A wise servant is always so."

"Servant!"

"Servant. If Lady Silverthorne does not hire me, I must seek employment elsewhere, and soon. If she does, I will be a servant here."

"If you are the owner of that necklace, and I am nearly sure that you are, soon you will be quite wealthy."

She shook her head. "It is an expensive bauble, no doubt, one I could never hope to purchase with a lifetime of earnings. But at the same time, its sale would hardly make me wealthy."

"Thorne thinks it worth several thousands, perhaps ten thousand pounds."

Penny blanched and shoved the box at him. He chuckled and put it in the safe, closing the door and checking to see that it latched firmly.

"That puts a different face on matters, doesn't it?"

She frowned. "I can't imagine that Lord Silverthorne would give such a costly thing to someone he hardly knows, for no better reason than a bit of armament falling to the floor."

"And Allison's undisturbed night's sleep."

"One night? I do pray her bad dreams stop, but if they do, I believe it will have more to do with feeling less alone in her situation than with any spirits that might exist."

"You simply won't accept that they exist, will you?"

"I would do so with the greatest reluctance."

He smiled down at her approvingly, making her head spin somehow. "Consistent in your principles. I like that. Well, time will tell. If Allison sleeps well tonight . . ."

She shrugged and walked out of the room, saying, as she went, "It proves nothing, really."

When she gained the foyer, she paused. Where was she going? What was she going to do? She had never had nothing to do before, and found herself at a complete loss.

"Would you like to see the castle?"

She jumped, not realizing Mr. Betterton had come up behind her.

"What? Oh. I've seen it."

"No, you've seen one face of it. Aren't you curious to visit the scene of—"

"So much carnage? No. In fact, I find the idea most unpleasant."

"Oh. Well, would you like to go riding?"

"I don't ride."

"Don't ride?"

She spun toward him. "I am a governess, sir. I teach children their alphabet, the globe, and arithmetic. Also music and art and, if possible, an appreciation of literature. But riding is outside my purview, so I have never been instructed in it. And short of sitting astride half-wild Welsh ponies when a little girl, I have never had the opportunity of learning it on my own."

James rocked back on his heels at her vehemence. "Sorry. I meant no insult."

"No, of course, you didn't. I apologize for my tone of voice. I suppose I am a bit overset. I think I'll find out whether little Lord Riggswheel is prospering. Perhaps Lady Silverthorne would want me to take him for an outing."

"Good idea! Little knacker loves to go outside and run about. I'll go, too." He turned toward the family butler, who hovered nearby. "Grimsby, have Cook pack us a picnic, will you?"

Penny's cheeks flamed. She had been trying to avoid spending time with Mr. Betterton and now he proposed spending the afternoon with her. But she had to face the fact that Mr. Betterton was very much a part of this household, and to learn to deal with him calmly.

"Very well, if his parents approve."

"Oh, they'll approve. Jason runs circles around his fat old nanny. They'll be glad for us to work some of the fidgits out of him, and so will she."

They met Lord Silverthorne coming down the stairs from the nursery, a relieved look on his face. When James explained their mission, he said he thought it was an excellent idea.

"He was most incensed that he couldn't play with his mother, and then he wanted me to entertain him, which I would love to do, but I have some pressing estate business."

"A walk, a romp, and a picnic, and he'll be ready for his nap," James said. "You'd best change shoes, Miss Jones. Have you any half boots?"

She did, and watched Mr. Betterton take the stairs two at a time up to his second-cousin's quarters. Something about his athletic energy made her smile.

"A wild pair, Miss Jones. Don't let them wear you out," Lord Silverthorne said, grinning.

"I have younger siblings. I am an old hand at keeping up." They walked down the stairs together, and he left her at her door with his thanks. She not only changed shoes, but she also put on her oldest dress. It was a most unattractive garment, and she donned it like armor, sure it would keep Mr. Betterton's thoughts from straying away from his little relative.

It was her own thoughts she repeatedly had to keep from straying, as Mr. Betterton romped in the grass with Lord Riggswheel while the Nanny looked on. She and a broad-shouldered footman had accompanied them, the latter bearing a heavy picnic basket. The sturdy four-year-old shrieked with laughter as he rode Betterton's strong back, and even more when he was bucked off. He hung on desperately, using his "horsie's" hair for purchase, bringing mock bellows of rage from James.

Penny sat on a blanket under a wide spreading oak tree and watched the two romp, smiling broadly herself at the sight of such uninhibited joy. When invited to participate in ring around the rosy, she did so without pausing to consider the possible consequences, so she had no one but herself to blame when she tumbled down right next to Mr. Betterton. Before she could scramble up, Jason threw himself across the two of them and declared himself the winner.

"What game were we playing, you young varmint?" James picked him up and held him high in the air.

"King of the world. And I'm king, because I'm the highest."

"How high are you?" James asked.

"As high as ever I can be," the boy declared, giggling.

"I don't think so, do you, Miss Jones?"

He looked over at her and winked. Her heart did an odd somersault. Realizing she had remained lying right by Mr. Betterton's side, she hastily sat up and scooted away.

"Well, he seems pretty high to me."

"No, I'm not. I can go higher. Show her, Uncle James."

"Very well." James raised his legs and tucked them under the boy. Obviously they had played this game before, because Jason maneuvered his stomach onto James's feet quite expertly.

"Now. Ready? Up!" James raised his legs straight into the air, brandishing the boy above him.

"See, Miss Jones. Now I'm really, really high."

"You are indeed." She smiled.

James reached his hands up to steady the boy. "Ready?"

"Yes!"

"OK. Up!" And he bounced the boy into the air. The few inches seemed like miles to the child, who shrieked enthusiastically and cried, "Do it again!"

His cousin accommodated him several times, then slowly lowered his legs to the ground, setting the boy on his feet.

"More," Jason yelled, running around and landing on James's chest.

"No, you miscreant. I'm worn-out! And we're leaving Miss Jones out of our games."

"I bet you can lift her on your feet." Jason tugged at Penny's hand. "Come on, let's see."

Penny laughed and stood up. "I don't think I am brave enough for that game." Catching the boy around the waist, she spun around several times with her arms extended, laughing as much as he did as he whooshed through the air. When she had to stop for dizziness's sake, Jason joined her on the grass, leaning against her.

"You're fun. Isn't she, Uncle James?"

"She certainly is."

Something in Mr. Betterton's voice made her look at him sharply. His eyes were shining with mischief again. She realized how she must have looked, spinning around so wildly. Perhaps he had seen her ankles. Certainly her hair must be all atumble.

"Blushes become you," he said, sitting beside her. Jason climbed on his back. "No, you don't. Time to rest awhile." He reached behind himself and lifted the boy over, throwing him across his lap and tickling him into submission. Silence reigned as Jason caught his breath. Abruptly his smile turned to a sad little frown.

"I wish Mommy was fun like she used to be," he said. "She never romps with me now."

"She will again one day soon," James assured him, smoothing the boy's hair from his eye. "Now rest a bit so your tummy won't be too dizzy to eat lunch."

"OK. Tell me a story."

"Let's see if Miss Jones knows any stories."

Penny cocked her head and thought. "Yes, I do know a story. It's about a frog."

She proceeded to tell a story that involved hand gestures and frog noises and made no sense whatsoever, but which had always amused her younger siblings.

"Why did the frog eat a fly?" Jason asked, making a face.

"Oh, didn't you know? To frogs, flies taste as good as seed cakes do to us."

"Really? I would like to try a fly."

The two adults exchanged looks of alarm.

"Not a good idea," James told the boy. "To you, a fly would taste like the bottom of an old boot."

"What does that taste like?"

"Hmmm." Penny thought she'd best bring this line of thought to a close before the child embarked on a series of unsavory experiments. "Like very bitter medicine. Have you ever had bitter medicine?"

"Yes. I had a fever last month. Nurse gave me some horrid green stuff on a spoon."

"Yes, well, that's what flies and old boots taste like."

"Oh. Well, I guess I'll have seed cakes." He got up and went to the picnic basket, presided over by his nanny, who had fallen asleep on her blanket next to it.

"Phew. Good thinking," James said.

Penny laughed. "Practice! Remember, I have younger brothers."

The "little picnic" was an elaborate meal. By the time she had eaten her fill, Penny was as sleepy as Jason, who stretched out beside his lethargic nanny and fell asleep.

James smiled at her. "You look as if you would like to join them there."

"It is tempting. But I haven't slept in the daytime since—well, I can't remember when. I am not accustomed to being idle, either. Much more of it will give me the fidgits."

"I feel the same way. There are things that I need to do at Fairmont. I expect I had best be on my way in a day or two."

"Where is Fairmont?" She should be glad he was leaving. Why did the thought make her sad?

"About half a day's ride east of here. I'm building a new house there. It's almost completed. It will have steam heating and water closets on every floor. Everything the most modern and up-to-date."

"Gaslights, too?"

"No, alas. Unless I build my own gas plant and lines, that improvement will not be possible. I thought about it, but there's no good place to set up the plant that wouldn't spoil my view. Fairmont has the most beautiful view in England, I believe. It is set on a hill, looking down on the Wye River."

Penny smiled and listened to his enthusiastic description of his new home, and to his plans for improving the soil and livestock in imitation of Coke of Norfolk. She was surprised to hear him so eloquent on the subject of improved cattle and swine and the attributes of various kinds of plows.

"I am sure I am boring you," he said suddenly.

"No, indeed. I am most impressed. I had thought you . . . I mean . . ."

He laughed. "Lady Hartnet certainly filled your head with tales of my wild youth. I am a changed man from then, Miss Jones. No more pranks and raking about. I am seeking a wife, and mean to be true to her."

"It is a pity she was so prejudiced against you. Her older daughter, Mary, might have suited you very well."

"I thought she might at the time, but I am finding my notions of a wife changing." The look he gave her made Penny's heart turn over.

She primmed her lips together. "Next season, you will find the right woman, I am sure. I think I will go back to the house. I need to write my father."

He begged her, "Don't go. Tell me about your family. How many siblings do you have?"

"Eleven. No. Ten." She felt color rising in her cheeks and turned away.

"Lost one, then?" His voice held sympathy. "I am an only child. My mother had two others but they did not survive infancy. It was very hard for all of us."

She nodded, holding back tears. "Lost. Yes, I lost a sister. I have two younger sisters and the rest are brothers. All are half siblings, but I don't look at them that way. I adore my stepmother. She never made a difference between me and her birth children, and is ever cheerful though it is very hard to raise such a numerous family on an impecunious parson's stipend."

"Hence your sending most of your salary away while looking for another position. I admire your love for your family, but confess I question the good sense of not holding back more money for yourself. You looked half starved in London. Starting to fill out now. The bloom is back."

Penny grew increasingly uncomfortable with this conversation. "You and Lord and Lady Silverthorne seem almost like siblings."

"Yes, it is a close relationship now. When we were young, we were close because our fathers were friends as well as relations. Then Lydia Kiesley, Agatha's sister, married Thorne's father. She wanted all of his attention, and drove a wedge between him and everyone who cared for him. Since the day we found the treasure, though, we've been thick as inkle weavers."

"I don't feel so well," a small voice piped up.

James instantly picked Jason up and put him in his lap, where he held a hand against the child's cheek. "He doesn't seem feverish."

Penny touched Jason's other cheek. "No, he doesn't. I expect he just had a bit more to eat than was good for him. We'd best take him back to the nursery."

"A dose of calomel will do him up fine," the nanny asserted, emerging from her near stupor after eating an enormous lunch.

Penny shook her head. "He doesn't need anything strong. Just rest and some quiet time."

"I expect I know what he needs," the nanny asserted. She struggled to her feet. "Come along, young master. A good purging and you'll feel fine."

"I don't want to!"

James stood. "I know nothing of children, but I think we should consult Lady Silverthorne before dosing him."

The nanny looked mulish, but could only bow her head. Penny and James left her and the footman to deal with the remains of the picnic, and hastened back to the house with Jason.

"I do hope Lady Silverthorne will allow me to have the care of him. I wonder at the competence of that woman."

"As do I."

They made their way to Thorne Hall, and laid the case, and the boy, before Allison, who took him into her bed, for she was still lying down, and had called them into her bedchamber.

"Some peppermint and honey is what I prescribe," she said, tucking the boy under the covers next to her.

This met with Jason's approval, as well as Penny's and James's. The boy snuggled down by his mother, and James went off to get the required dose from Cook.

Penny went to her room to begin her letter to her father. But her mind kept straying to the afternoon spent with James and Jason. She thought she could never recall a time of more unalloyed pleasure than that.

I will miss him, she thought. *May he leave soon.*

It was hard to write the letter to her father. She had to keep skirting around Mr. James Betterton, and the effect he had on her, when she strongly wished to blurt it out. It would only upset and alarm her father, though. She now knew she was in no danger of rape or deliberate seduction from this formerly notorious young man, but it would be impossible for someone who had not met him and come to know him to believe he had truly reformed.

It was a long letter. She crossed her lines as

usual, but did not recross them, for she felt sure
the marquess would frank what had grown into a
small packet, almost, by the time she was finished.
She hoped her father would reply quickly, to give
her some guidance on the supposed ghosts.

She wished she could tell him the Silverthornes
had hired her, but no such offer had been forthcoming yet. In view of all the strange events, that
detail had as yet escaped their attention. *I will try
to hint at the matter this evening after dinner,* she
thought as she started to change into evening wear.
Jane rushed into the room just as she was putting
her hair into a simple knot.

"Oh, miss, you should have rung for me."

"I am sorry. I am so accustomed to doing for
myself. But your help with my hair will be greatly
appreciated."

This pleased the maid no end, and she sculpted
a very elegant style for Penelope.

"Jane, have you seen a bound sheaf of papers
that was in my baggage?"

The maid turned cherry red. "Oh, I do be sorry,
ma'am. I was putting it away and happened to open
it. I saw the pretty drawings. That's what caught
my eye. I knew it wasn't a diary, or it would have
been locked away. I wasn't snooping."

"No, of course not." She smiled at the maid. *No
wonder they always say there are no secrets from
servants.* "But where is it?"

Jane grew even redder, if possible. "It is under
my pillow. I was reading it. Or trying to. I do think
I could learn to read with such a book as that. It
is meant to be a book, miss?"

Penny frowned a little. She was torn between

chastising the maid and being flattered that she would find the illustrated alphabet poem helpful.

"Yes, it is meant to be a book someday. Would you bring it to me please? I wish to show it to Lady Silverthorne and ask her permission to show it to Lord Riggswheel. You may look at it again later. In fact, I will go over it with you and help you figure out the parts you don't understand."

"You would? Oh, ma'am!" Jane clapped her hands together. "That would be ever so nice. I wasn't going to steal it. You see that. I was going to bring it back."

"Of course you were."

"Whoever wrote and drew that little book is a godsend to those who'd like to learn their letters. I mean, it is for children, but still . . ."

"I'm pleased to hear you say that, for I wrote and illustrated it. But the dinner bell will sound soon, so would you . . . ?"

She had no sooner mentioned the dinner bell than Jane left the room on a run. Penny was astonished at how quickly she returned from the servant's quarters, for she knew they must be at least two floors above her. Puffing from her exertion, Jane delivered the book with another apology, which Penny waved off, for now she must hasten. She hoped to reach the drawing room ahead of Agatha and present the book to Lord and Lady Silverthorne. If they were impressed with it, perhaps she could secure for herself the post of governess.

Chapter Nine

*U*nbeknownst to Penny, James had stayed behind with Allison for a private conversation. As soon as Jason had fallen asleep, he drew his chair up next to the bed and whispered to her, "Allie, will you please hire Miss Jones for your governess?"

Allison frowned a little. "I don't know."

"But . . . but you like her, don't you?"

"I like her very well, but so do you."

"That is why I need you to get her to stay here. Otherwise, she'll seek a position elsewhere. Oh, Allie, if you could have seen her with Jason. She finally let down her guard with me today. She has a million-candle smile. Such a way with the boy. And wise, too. Wouldn't think of letting your nanny dose Jason with calomel."

"This is not about Jason, though."

He shook his head. "I think she is the one, Allie. I've been drawn to her ever since I met her, and now I do believe I've found my match."

"I am very glad for you, but hiring her as a servant raises problems. For one thing, what excuse will you give for seeing her? In the ordinary way of things, your paths would not cross overmuch."

"You could still have her dine with us when you are dining *en famille*. After all, the librarian and the estate manager do."

"But how long will you be able to stay here without giving your interest away to Thorne?"

"He suspects anyway. Why should I care if he knows? I'll tell him myself."

"You know how very reprehensible Thorne finds it when men of our class involve themselves with servants."

James's face fell. "Oh! That's right. But I don't think of her as a servant. Do you?"

"Not now. But you can't get away from the fact that that is what she would be as a governess. And she would be very much on her guard again, I suspect, because of her previous unpleasant experience. I think it would be better for your sake *not* to engage her as a servant."

James nodded, his brow furrowed. "Then how are we to keep her here?"

Allison had no ready answer for that. "I think, if you wish to court her, you had best ask Thorne for his cooperation."

James turned his head to one side, worry lines furrowing his brow. "If he says no . . ."

"You will simply have to convince him. I won't go behind his back."

James sighed. "Sometimes it seems we have put that whole guardianship thing behind us, but other times I feel very much the rebellious youth he tried to dominate, with such unsatisfactory results."

"Do you want me to talk to him first?"

"I . . . Let me think about it. I don't want to hide behind your petticoat."

"Very well. But we have to decide soon, for as

you say, if we don't hire her, she'll be on her way. She is in need of a position, and also is not one to sit about doing nothing, I think."

"Just so. Well, that settles it. I am going to talk to Thorne about it, man to man, and try to gain his cooperation. He'll have to go away, you see."

"Go away?" Allison sat up in the bed, her voice loud enough to make Jason mumble in his sleep.

"Shhh. Yes. Don't you see? He needs to go to some of his estates anyway. With you increasing, what would be more natural than that I would drop in on you often? And stay for extended periods? Of course, that will be after he has hired her. If she gets wind of it first, she'll bolt."

"Oh, James, I don't know."

"Now he always travels around to his various holdings at this time of year."

"That's true. And ordinarily he would take me, but that's impossible this year."

"So I'd actually be doing him a favor."

Allison grinned at him. "In a way, you would."

"That's it, then. I'm on my way down to talk to him."

"I'd really like to help you, James, but I don't think it will work. As you told me, Miss Jones reacted very negatively when you first tried to hire her, for no better reason than that you might run tame here. She has reason for being wary."

"That was before she knew me. Surely she wouldn't fear me now."

"If I hire her, then immediately decamp, with you remaining in residence, it would look most suspicious."

"I don't intend to remain. I do intend to return

after you have departed, to look in on Allie. Nothing odd about that."

Thorne considered a moment, then shook his head. "Besides, I do not like the idea of you courting a servant. Give me a little time to think of something else."

"Not too much time. Allie agrees with me that she will not stay without promise of a position."

"Understood. And I don't want her to leave until I am sure that ghost is gone. I haven't any reason not to hire her, except for the one reason you most want her to stay." Thorne sighed, and his regret was so palpable James could not work up any resentment. They repaired to the drawing room to wait for dinner to be served.

To their surprise, Agatha and Mr. Bartholomew had not yet put in an appearance, though Allison awaited them.

"Pure bliss," Thorne said, glancing around the room before giving his wife a quick kiss.

She smiled up at him. "Indeed. Oh, here is Miss Jones."

Penny's heart pounded as she hurried up to the group. Her very future could depend upon this moment. She wanted to make her move before the odious Miss Kiesley arrived, so she held out her manuscript to Allison.

"Why, what is this? Oh, delightful!" Allison quickly turned the pages. "Jason will love this."

"I have a dozen more similar books in Wales. I can have father send them here if—that is, umm—I should very much like to be your son's governess."

Thorne took the book from his wife and exclaimed over it. "You say you have a dozen more! This is a little treasure! You should have such books published. What a blessing this would be in teaching beginners to read—a children's book that is cheerful, colorful, and humorous."

"I offered it to several publishers. They were very interested until I made it clear that I would not, could not, pay for the first printing. And it seems that with these colored illustrations the books would be far too dear for anyone but the very rich, so one could never recoup the investment."

Thorne considered the book carefully, going back over every page. "Hmmm." He looked at his cousin. "What do you think, James?"

James smiled at the humorous drawings. "I think it is a great pity these can't be made widely available."

"This may be exactly what we are looking for."

"Looking for?" Penny puzzled over this remark as the two cousins exchanged a look that seemed full of meaning.

Thorne turned to her, a wide smile on his face. "We three have been looking for a project. Haven't we, Allison?"

Allison wasn't quite sure what her husband was driving at, but quickly agreed.

"What you need is a patron, Miss Jones. Someone who can help you get your books printed and in the hands of children all over the country, rich or poor."

James nodded sagely. "Something to benefit mankind. We've been very fortunate, the three of us, what with finding that treasure and all. We've been looking for ways to share."

Allison enthusiastically joined in. "And this will be the perfect project to give some employment to our workers who are being displaced by farm machinery and changing crop patterns."

Penny felt a little lost. "How could my books benefit them?"

Allison took back the bound manuscript. "We could establish our own printing press and bindery on the estate. Also, the books don't have to be colored in such perfect naturalistic detail, as you have done, to interest children, do they? For instance, the leaves could just be green, and the pony a light brown instead of such sophisticated shading"—she looked anxiously up at Penny—"if you don't feel it would violate your artistic vision too much. Many people could be trained to do simple coloring once the book is printed."

"Oh. I see. Of course, that is just what one of the book publishers said, and I agreed to allow that. Then he quoted me a somewhat reduced price for printing the books. Little did he guess I had scarcely a guinea to my name!"

"We are not late, so you must be early." A strident female voice proclaimed the arrival of Agatha, closely followed by Mr. Bartholomew.

"We'll discuss this in more detail tomorrow," Lord Silverthorne said sotto voce. "Just the three of us. James, you can stay your departure one more day, can't you?"

James nodded enthusiastically. The estate agent and the librarian arrived, and minutes later the butler announced dinner.

Penny's mind was so befuddled by the three cousins' extreme interest in her book, she scarcely heard a word of conversation during dinner. She allowed herself to be coaxed into a game of whist afterward. She and Allison played Miss Kiesley and

Mr. Bartholomew, and got soundly trounced, which put Agatha in a slightly better mood than usual. Mr. Betterton and Lord Silverthorne had their heads together for quite a while during the evening, and then apologized and asked the ladies to play and sing for them before retiring.

Lady Silverthorne proved to be a virtuoso on the piano in a difficult piece by Mozart. She then played while Penny sang a couple of Thomas Moore's songs. The two men joined them for some other songs, and Penny felt warmed to her toes by James's rich baritone.

It was a pleasant evening, and she retired feeling very happy, until she climbed into bed and realized that her future looked as unsettled as ever. More so, perhaps, with new possibilities in sight. It took a long time to fall asleep, and almost immediately she began to dream of the maid wearing the ruby necklace.

This was different from any other dream, though. The maid was wrapped in her red cloak and paced back and forth on the rampart of the castle. Then she turned and looked directly at Penny and said, "You must come to Silverthorne Castle." This message was repeated over and over until Penny woke up. She wondered if Allison was having dreams again, or a ghost visitation.

I don't want to go to Silverthorne Castle. She didn't quite understand the dread that filled her at the very thought. She paced around the room a little before finally lying back down. At last fell she asleep again, not to wake until morning.

It was full light when she woke up. Surprised that the maid hadn't awakened her, Penny got out of bed and began to dress. Apparently Jane had been listening for signs of life, for she popped into the room, eager to assist Penny.

The breakfast room was uncharacteristically full when she went down. Lord and Lady Silverthorne were there, James, Agatha, Bartholomew, the librarian—everyone but the estate agent. Penny studied Allison's face surreptitiously as she ate, checking for any sign that she had had a bad night's sleep. But Allison looked well rested, and there was no talk of ghosts or necklaces around the table.

Agatha sat next to Mr. Bartholomew, discussing something in a low voice. Penny wondered at the intimacy of their tone and posture. She quickly turned her head away, only to meet Mr. Betterton's eyes. He winked at her, then looked meaningfully at the pair. She couldn't quite suppress a smile, though the last thing she wanted was intimate glances and shared secrets between herself and this attractive young man.

Lord and Lady Silverthorne sat together at the head of the table, quietly discussing the morning's newspapers. Abruptly Lord Silverthorne's voice rose. He was reading from the Morning Post.

> Strange events once more alarm the Silverthornes, as an ancient necklace has been discovered in the castle ruins, draped over the ribs of a skeleton. The valuable ruby necklace came complete with its own ghosts. No less than two of the specters have begun haunting the castle.
>
> Even stranger still, a young lady, one Miss Penelope Jones, who came to the castle to apply for the position of governess, now claims the necklace belongs to her by

right of inheritance from an ancestress of hers. This Miss Jones claims to have been dreaming for years about the necklace being about the neck of her forebear when she perished in the collapse of the castle's north wall. Friends of the Silverthornes fear that they are being imposed upon by an adventuress.

"I never have claimed ownership of that necklace," Penny exclaimed. She put her hands to her cheeks. "That story will be read all over Britain. My father will read it. Oh! This is dreadful."

"Of course you have never claimed the necklace," Allison said soothingly.

"Agatha, this story has your name all over it." Silverthorne glared at Miss Kiesley.

"It can't have! I never wrote that!"

"I suppose you have told no one about the necklace?"

"News of the necklace's discovery had already reached London when I left there."

"But no one but those at Thorne Manor knows of the connection with Miss Jones."

"There is no connection with Miss Jones. She is just an artful poseur, seeking to take advantage . . ."

"Again I say, you sent that story to the paper. How dare you. This time you have gone too far!"

"I didn't!" Agatha jumped up, tears in her eyes. "I swear it! I may have written of the situation to some friends of mine, but how was I to know they would tell the papers?"

Allison put a hand on her husband's arm. After a few tense moments, he settled back in his chair.

"I am very sorry about this, Miss Jones. I know

it is extremely embarrassing to you. But after all, our research may reveal that you are indeed descended from the original owner, and then—"

"I don't want it! I earn my own way in the world. I shan't take something I don't deserve."

"Ha! Pretty words!" Agatha glared at her.

Mr. Betterton came to Penny's defense, fire in his eyes. "You old harpy, stop insulting Miss Jones. I shan't let your jealousy cause her any more pain."

"Enough." Silverthorne arose and came to Penny's side. "When you have finished your breakfast, Miss Jones, would you meet with us in the bedroom the farthest to the west? We need to see if it meets your requirements for our new business venture."

Agatha's head came up and it was clear she was preparing an interrogation, so Penny rose immediately. "I am ready now, my lord."

"Good. James? Allison?"

The other two quickly followed them out of the breakfast room, leaving behind a frustrated, expostulating Agatha.

Mr. Bartholomew stood up and started to go with them, but Silverthorne stopped him at the door. "Go back to your breakfast. I do not require your services at this time."

"But, my lord, you mentioned business."

"If I need you, I will send for you."

Mr. Bartholomew retreated reluctantly back into the dining room.

James laughed aloud once they reached the stairs. "Why do I feel like a naughty child who has escaped my tutor?"

They all joined him in laughter, and it was a merry party that entered the southwestern bedroom. Penny was surprised to see that it was fitted up, not as a sleeping room, but with tables and easels.

"This is where Mr. Turner worked the summer he painted the castle and other views around Thorne Hall," Lord Silverthorne said. "He declared the light to be perfect for painting."

Penny surveyed the room. "It is. And a wonderful view from two different sides of the house. Oh! This is where he painted the view of the valley that hangs in your drawing room."

"Yes. Amazing how the artist's eye transforms a mundane rural scene into a transcendent masterpiece." Allison looked out the window and then turned to Penny, smiling. "I had a try at it, and my picture just looked like land and cows. Of course, you are a much better artist than I."

"I hope I am much too wise to attempt a view once the great J.M.W. Turner has painted it!"

The others laughed, and Lord Silverthorne motioned for them to be seated in a group of chairs around the fireplace. "It gets a little cold in here at night in the winter," he said. "But in the daytime, if there is sun, it warms up quite nicely. It isn't well suited as a bedroom, though, so we left it as is."

"A good thing, now," James said.

"Here is our idea, Miss Jones." All business, Lord Silverthorne drew her attention back to him. "We plan to establish a charitable foundation. We would like you to serve on the board of trustees."

"Me, a trustee?"

"Yes. Allison was already working on some education ideas before you came here."

"And I've been floundering, especially lately."

"What we need is a trained teacher to run our foundation. That will be in addition to your work on the books. We propose to offer you an honorarium adequate to replace any salary you would be forgoing. We think four hundred pounds per annum would be about right."

"Four hundred pounds? My lord, I . . ."

"And, of course, a royalty on your books, once published. You'll oversee the budget for having the books printed and distributed. Allison has a list of orphanages and small schools ready."

"But you may well locate others to add to it," Allison added.

"May I make a suggestion?" James asked.

"Of course." His cousin settled back in his chair so Penny could see Mr. Betterton clearly.

"The first edition of the books should be a small one, quite deluxe, which will be offered for sale to the *ton* at a premium price. That would help launch them into the world. Those who purchase them will be enchanted, and encourage others to buy them, and the proceeds would help print more books for the poor. Of course, our foundation will subsidize the latter."

"What do you think, Miss Jones?"

"It seems a very good plan. But I don't feel I could take a royalty on books you purchase to give away. After all, it *is* for charity. And it would feel as if I were being paid twice, if I am to receive a stipend for producing them."

The three cousins exchanged looks, then nodded their heads in agreement.

"How long do you think it would take you to prepare a dozen books for the printer, Miss Jones?"

"All of them? Several months, I fear. I learned something of the process for producing drawings suitable for engravings, and it would not be merely a matter of giving my little chapbooks to the printer."

"Oh, I am glad," Allison said. "I was afraid you'd have to go off to London right away, to purchase a printing press and a bindery. I have to confess I dread being left with Agatha as my only companion while Thorne is seeing to his other estates."

Penny felt a little thrill of unease run through her. "You don't have to go to such an extent to get me to stay," she said. "I am perfectly willing to work for you as your companion or governess, or both. This salary you are proposing—"

"Honorarium."

"Whatever you call it, it is far too generous."

Allison shook her head. "I doubt you will think so by the time you have shepherded these books through the printer's, talked them up among the *ton* next spring, and then produced the less expensive editions. That will involve hiring and training people from around here to color them."

"Don't forget, we are going to have them printed on the estate, or near it," Lord Silverthorne interjected.

Penny had the feeling of being swept along on a strong tide. "Perhaps we should have the first edition printed in London, and then if it is well received, you could make the investment in machinery and hire someone to train workers. I can begin training colorists then, too. I would hate to jump ahead with material for several books, and have you pour money into equipment, if the books aren't going to succeed."

"They will succeed," James declared.

"I think so, too. Still, it is a very good point. Now didn't I say she would know what to do?" Allison leaned over and clasped Penny's hand, smiling broadly. "And from now on, you are to call me and Thorne and James by our first names. After all, we are colleagues, working together for a worthy goal."

Colleagues? Penny looked from one to the other, and wondered if she could be so informal with these people. They were trying to make her feel like an equal, but she knew better. The gap between them could never be bridged. Clearly they thought differently, or wished her to think they did. It crossed her mind that there was something a bit fishy about the whole proposition. But four hundred pounds per annum! She could send money to John in school, to the family in Wales, and perhaps even put a little away for herself.

All of that and a chance to do something so beneficial for so many children! How could she refuse? In fact . . . A daring idea came to her. Would they laugh at her, or worse yet be angered by the suggestion? She decided to put to the test their pretense of working *with* her rather than merely hiring her.

"I wonder. Once we have produced the children's books, would you consider adding books that would help adults learn to read with little or no formal instruction? Or would that be going too far? Some people object to the lower orders learning to read, but if you advocate educating poor children, surely you don't think so."

"A capital idea," James exclaimed.

"Agreed. It would be difficult to do, though, wouldn't it?" Thorne looked inquiringly at her.

"I believe the right pictures could be used to bridge the gap between the written and spoken word," Penny said.

The four of them spent the rest of the morning talking over ideas for their educational foundation, and by the end of that time, Penny had lost all inhibitions about offering her own ideas, as the others seemed very receptive. Best of all, when one or the other of them disagreed with her suggestions, they said so, which reassured Penny that they weren't pandering to her for some reason.

At last Allison stood up and stretched. "It is more than time for some food. What do you all say to a picnic on such a beautiful day? It would be a good farewell to James. We can take Jason."

"Though we won't let the little nipper stuff himself so this time," James laughed.

Penny smiled and stood up herself. "It sounds like an excellent plan to me." Though some part of her was saddened to see James leave, her last reservation about the whole book scheme fell away when she learned he was really going. A niggling fear had eaten at her all morning long. She knew she was attracted to the handsome young man, and he to her. Being thrown together in terms of such equality that she let her guard down was a recipe for disaster.

"Wonderful. We'll go to the castle. After we eat, we can go up on the ramparts. You'll love the view from there, Penny. I'm sure you'll want to take your sketching pad." Allison started for the door.

A strong sense of dread washed over Penny. "The castle!"

Chapter Ten

*T*he astonished looks in Allison's and Thorne's eyes made Penny feel like sinking into the ground.

"What, you do not wish to see our castle, Miss . . . that is, Penny?" Thorne looked puzzled, and a little insulted.

"Never mind," Allison said. "We don't have to go there. But it is entirely safe now, you know. Thorne has had extensive work done to shore up the structure and his workers are now rebuilding the north wall. That area is fenced off. We'll go into the center, near the keep, for our picnic, and later Thorne and James can take Jason up on the ramparts—he loves the view. If you do not care to go up there, I will show you the old keep with its fine chapel, one of the few that survived the civil wars intact.

"It . . . it sounds lovely," Penny said.

"She is pale as a sheet." James crossed to her and knelt by her chair. He lifted Penny's limp hands and chafed them to warm them up. "I think her dreams have given her a dread of the place."

Both surprised and pleased at James's sensitivity to her feelings, Penny nodded. "I have dreamed of the collapse of those walls so often, it seems like a recent event. But I will make myself go."

"Nonsense." James looked at his cousin. "Let us go down to the lake instead. We can get in a bit of fishing afterward, Thorne."

The others agreed. She appreciated James making it easy on her to avoid the castle. She also felt a little guilty for refusing the opportunity to go there, when her dream the night before told her that is exactly what she must do.

Later, a sturdy, open farm wagon pulled up to the door to Thorne Manor, and Penny watched as picnic baskets, blankets, and iced buckets of ale were loaded in the back. When Jason arrived, Thorne took the reins, the boy sandwiched between him and James. Allison and Penny sat on the backseat.

When Jason realized their destination was not the castle, he began to fuss. "I want to see the geese," he exclaimed. "I want to go up on the ramparts and see forever."

"Not today, son," Thorne said. "Now behave, or we will leave you behind."

"Geese?" Penny looked at Allison for explanation.

"Yes. There is a flock up there that serve as very effective watchdogs. The appearance of a stranger sets them to squawking. They can be heard all the way down to the manor.

"I want to feed the geese today." Jason stood on the seat and looked back at his mother. She smiled and patted his cheek.

"You enjoy the lake, too. We can see the turtles sunning themselves."

The little boy thrust out his lower lip. A tear trickled down his cheek.

Penny could not stand it. "I think Jason is right. This is a perfect day to go to the castle."

The others all looked skeptically at her. "Are you sure?" James asked.

"Yes. I am going to be living here for quite a while, it seems. I must become accustomed. I mustn't be a coward."

"Goody!" Jason jumped up and down and clapped his hands. His father, with one last look at Penny to be sure she meant what she said, clicked his tongue at the horses, a pair of sturdy farm animals, and guided them along the road that had brought Penny to Thorne Hall. She gazed up at the looming castle, admiring the ancient building. From this side it looked perfect.

"Are those stairs?"

"Yes, stone steps carved from the cliff face, with some wooden stairs here and there, make it possible to climb up to the castle from behind the manor house. It is for the vigorous, of course, but is much faster than going by the roads." Allison began telling her of the time that she had climbed those stairs at night, with only the glow made by the ghost of the Silver Lady to guide her.

"You're so brave," Penny said. "I find heights very unsettling."

"Must be difficult in Wales," Thorne observed.

"True. I was always less enthusiastic about climbing the hills and mountains for the views, even though I enjoyed them immensely when I finally got up there. And got the courage to look," she added with a laugh.

Their route to the castle led back toward the post road. A turnoff Penny had not noticed on arrival led uphill between a stand of ancient trees so thickly arched over the roadway it seemed they were passing through a dark green tunnel. Penny noted with interest that the trees on the cliff side of the road actually grew from several feet below road level. An abrupt drop-off along the road hinted of an old earth slip that had dropped a goodly chunk of land below road level, without destroying the ancient trees.

In spite of her misgivings, Penny felt no sense of danger at the castle. In fact, she found it a very peaceful place, once the gatekeeper had penned in the noisy geese. He did so with the help of the delighted little boy, who clearly loved throwing down their corn from the safety of his father's arms. Grass had been planted on what had once been the courtyard. A few trees provided shade, and the hilltop breeze was moderated by the ramparts, making the area cool but not windy.

After their picnic, the men announced plans to view the countryside from the ramparts. Penny declined their offer to take her along, waving Jason goodbye as he bounced eagerly on his uncle's shoulders. She thoroughly enjoyed the tour Allison gave her of the castle keep and the lovely chapel attached. She listened with interest to the story of the Silver Lady, who had led Allison and Thorne to the fabulous treasure beneath the castle.

"And Lord . . . I mean, Thorne . . . saw the ghosts here, too?" she asked Allison in wonderment.

"Yes. They took their farewell from us dressed very formally, right here in the chapel. Once their obligation to deliver the treasure to its rightful heirs had been met, they were free to move on."

Penny frowned and bowed her head. "Move on to what, I wonder."

"They seemed so serene, even joyful, to be leaving us at last, that I cannot doubt they thought their future would be a happy one."

"My father always denied ghosts could exist because Christ said to the repentant thief on the cross, 'This night you shall dwell with me in heaven.' So he thought the soul went immediately to its reward."

James startled them by entering the conversation. She had not realized he had rejoined them. "Could it not have been meant for that particular person and situation? Aren't there other passages that refer to the dead sleeping until the return of Christ?"

"I am embarrassed to say that I am not sure. I am guilty of taking my father's words as truth, I suppose, without critical thinking."

Allison joined in. "I never thought that passage had to be interpreted as applying to everyone. I think the Catholics have a good notion with their purgatory."

"I think that in Catholic teaching, purgatory is a place of punishment for sins, not at all pleasant, and its only desirable aspect is that it is not for eternity. At least"—she laughed a little self-consciously—"at least, that is what my father says."

James shrugged. "I yield to you on that point. Not much of a theologian. But I still say there's room for belief in ghosts, without denying or abrogating anything in the Bible."

Penny considered the matter. "Perhaps there is.

I can now no longer dismiss them out of hand—that is for sure."

Thorne entered the chapel, his sleeping son draped over his shoulder. "I think we'd best go home and tuck the little fellow in bed."

So they returned to the wagon. The gatekeeper had thoughtfully collected their picnic things already. James took the reins, joking about never wishing for any of his friends to see him driving so ordinary a vehicle.

"And such spirited cattle, too," Allison laughed. "It wouldn't do a thing for your reputation as a nonpareil to be caught driving calm old Dobbins and Sally."

"Half-dead old Dobbins," James pretended disgust.

"Not Dobbins," a sleepy child's voice piped up. "His name is Stockings."

"I do beg your pardon," James said, laughing.

"Go back by the back road, cousin James. I want to see the pretty lady who waves to me there."

"Pretty lady?" James looked at Thorne for elucidation.

"Don't ask me. First time he's ever mentioned it. Doubtless one of the estate workers."

"No, for she has jewels in her hair. Her clothes are funny, though."

Allison and Thorne exchanged puzzled, somewhat worried looks, but James had already turned down the back road. It ran on treeless, stony ground. Penny could see that the road curved gently ahead and then began a descent to the flatter land, where the hall stood.

"Anyway, it's a little shorter," he said somewhat defensively when Thorne scowled at him.

Penny felt her throat tightening. This road would doubtless lead them around to a point where she could see the north wall. She mentally braced herself for the experience. *Best get it over with,* she thought.

Allison leaned over and covered Penny's clenched hands, patting them gently, a gesture that made Penny feel warmly grateful. She forced herself to look as the carriage proceeded on the slowly curving road. Only a few trees stood between the road and the castle. At the moment the north wall came into view she could not hold back the gasp of recognition.

"You see her, too, don't you, Miss Jones?" Jason was wide-awake now, standing between Thorne and James and looking back at her. "Wave to her, Mommy, Miss Jones." And he set them an example, waving gaily.

Penny shook her head and looked to Allison for her cue. It was clear from Allison's expression that she also did not see anyone, but she waved, so Penny did likewise. Then she forced herself once again to confront the north wall of the castle.

"It is different," she blurted out.

"Different from your dreams?"

"Yes, and different from your painting, the one I saw in London." *The one that started this whole weird experience,* she thought to herself.

"Now that the structural repairs have been completed, returning the wall to its intact state is my goal," Thorne explained. "When my estate workers are idled by the season during late fall, and even during the winter when the weather allows, I hire them to make repairs under the supervision of an engineer, using stones from the collapsed wall to restore the north face to its original appearance. We are about half done."

"That process is what uncovered the necklace."

"Yes. We have recovered other—ah—remains, and small items of value have been found from time to time. But the necklace is the most spectacular such find."

Penny, absorbed in what she was seeing and comparing it with the castle in her dreams, did not notice what Jason was doing until he landed right in her lap, after climbing over the front seat into the back. She reflexively put her arms around him, and he snuggled against her.

"Why does the lady keep doing that?" he asked, looking up into her face. "She's never done it before."

"What?"

The boy made a beckoning motion. "It seems as if she wants us to stop and talk with her. Can we, Mother?"

Allison shook her head. "Not today. It is past time for your nap."

"I know. Nurse will be cross. Will you come back to see her later, Miss Jones?"

"Me?"

"Yes. I think she wants to talk to you."

Penny searched his mother's eyes for cues, but Allison looked both nervous and perplexed.

"Perhaps I will, someday. When we get home, would you like me to read you a story I made up, before you go to sleep? It has pictures as well as words. You might even be able to read most of it yourself, for the pictures show how different letters make different sounds."

"I like to read," the boy said, successfully distracted. "I can count to twenty, too. What comes after twenty-nine? Is it twenty-ten?"

Penny managed to keep the boy chattering about his alphabet and numbers until they returned to Thorne Hall. Stopping only to collect her book, she followed Thorne up the stairs, but by the time they reached Jason's room he had fallen asleep. His father tucked him in, and once they had quietly shut the door, leaving him in the care of the nanny, Thorne smiled down at her.

"Very glad you got him off the subject of that ghost."

"I am, too. If it is the same woman I see in that place in my dreams, I would not want the boy to witness any more of that drama. It would be horrifying to him."

"As it has been to you, each time you have dreamed it." Thorne sighed as they walked down the stairs. "I fear we were rather insensitive, taking you to the castle."

"It was at my request. If I am to live and work here much of the time, I must face the castle and adjust to it. But I do hope we can find some way to send these ghosts on to their reward—or punishment, as the case may be—before they frighten your child."

"Not half as much as I hope for it, I can assure you."

Though she had just written her father yesterday, Penny could not resist sending another note for the whole family, letting them know of her good fortune. They would be as pleased as she, and for the same reasons. She would earn a salary sufficient to assist them with their finances.

* * *

It was time for dinner by the time she finished her note. *Fortunately Lord Silverthorne can frank my correspondence,* she thought. Two such long letters in as many days would hit her father's purse rather hard otherwise.

She rang for Jane, who helped her put on her second-best evening dress. Jane once again did a magnificent job of arranging her hair. When she had finished, she opened the drawer of the small dressing table.

"I'll just help you put your cross on, shall I?" Jane reached for the velvet pouch where this small but precious ornament was kept, and lifted it out of the drawer wide-eyed with wonder.

"It do be heavy tonight. I 'spect you had some more jewelry in your baggage?"

Mystified, Penny took the pouch from the maid. "No, indeed. I can't imagine . . . Oh!" She drew from the bulging bag an astonishing quantity of tangled gold and rubies. It took a minute or two to tease the necklace into shape.

"I wonder how this got in here. You didn't put it here?"

"No, miss," Jane said, eyeing the necklace warily. "Do that be the ghost necklace?"

Penny smiled. "The necklace is not ghostly at all. It is very real. But it *is* the one that was found in the castle ruins. I wonder how it came to be in my jewelry pouch."

"Could be that ghost put it there." Jane backed away, wringing her hands together. "D-do you need me to put it on?"

Penny frowned. "Of course not. I don't plan to wear it. I plan to return it to the marquess."

"Oh. Well, can't say as I blame you. I'd not want that thing on my neck."

A thought occurred to Penny. "Even so, will you hold it for a moment while I pull out my own chain and cross?" She placed the necklace in the girl's hands without waiting for her consent and noticed that, though Jane's hands shook a little, she showed no signs of discomfort. She put on her jewelry and then took the necklace back.

"You did not find it uncomfortable to hold?"

"No, miss. A little scary. But it is as you say. Just stones and gold. Not the least ghostly."

Penny nodded, wondering what it meant that the girl had not felt the discomfort evinced by the Silverthornes and Agatha.

She carried the necklace downstairs, and entered the drawing room with it draped over her left hand.

"The nerve of that little baggage! How dare she take your necklace for her own!" Agatha's glance was as fiery as the red glowing stones in Penny's hand.

Chapter Eleven

"**D**on't be a ninny, Agatha. If she were stealing the necklace, she'd hardly be carrying it into Thorne's drawing room." James smiled at Penny encouragingly.

"I agree with you, though I think you could express yourself more politely," Thorne said, motioning Penny into the room. "I confess I am curious, though. How did you get that?"

"I thought perhaps you might know. It was in my jewelry pouch when my maid reached for my cross."

"How should I know?"

"Who else has the combination to the safe?"

"James and Allison," he answered, quizzing each of them with a glance, and receiving shakes of their heads for answer.

"Surely the ghost couldn't have . . ." Allison had an odd, laughing expression in her eyes.

"Hmmm. It is possible, I suppose. They can throw things and trip people and make shields fall off walls. I am beginning to believe they mean for you to have the necklace, Miss Jones." Thorne's eyes, too, glinted with amusement.

"That is just what she wishes you to believe, the scheming little—"

"Agatha," Allison said in a warning tone.

"Mr. Swinton, how is your research coming?" Thorne turned to the librarian.

"Very interesting. The Iltrys trace their lineage to a supposed royal bastard of Charles I, a Miss Charlotte de Quay, who married Mr. Iltry in 1665. Subsequently one of their descendants received a baronetcy. If either Miss de Quay or Mr. Iltry descended from this Lady Winifred, that would explain the connection to you, Miss Jones. Perhaps Miss de Quay was this Lady Winifred's child by the ill-fated king. The Iltrys had half a dozen children, three boys, three girls. You were, I suspect, descended from the youngest of the girls. But we need your mother's genealogy chart to confirm that."

"Well done, Swinton!" Thorne clapped him on the shoulder.

Penny looked at the valuable jewelry in her hands. "I have requested that Father send it, or a copy of it. But I doubt I am the only heiress of such a prolific family."

"Our ghosts seem to think you are a satisfactory recipient." Thorne winked at her.

"Well, I won't be satisfied until it is proven. Would you return this to the safe, my lord?"

Penny stretched and yawned as she awoke the next morning. She had slept well, with no dreams. She hoped Allison had done so as well. Her maid not being in sight, Penny unbraided her hair as she walked to the dresser. She started to open the drawer that held her comb and brush, when a sudden suspicion made her open the drawer holding the jewelry pouch instead. Sure enough, the pouch bulged and, when she tipped it, quickly disgorged the mass of rubies, diamonds, and gold chains.

She shook her head in wonderment. Was someone doing this for a trick? Could it really be spirits? She held the necklace up as if to put it on, just as the maid came in.

"Oh, my. I thought you left that downstairs."

"So did I. It seems to have turned up again. I think I will wear it to breakfast." She grinned. "I can't wait to hear Miss Kiesley's response to that!"

"A right piece of work is that one," the maid said, smiling. She helped Penny fasten the necklace as soon as she had dressed.

"A bit much for morning," Penny said, laughing at her reflection in the mirror.

When she walked into the breakfast room, only Miss Kiesley and Lord and Lady Silverthorne were there. With a pang, Penny remembered that James had planned to leave at daylight for his estate nearby.

Allison burst out laughing. Thorne muttered a mild expletive under his breath, but he was smiling. Agatha, predictably, squawked like a hen disturbed on her nest.

"That is that, then! The necklace is yours!" Thorne grinned at her.

"Oh, no! Not until there is proof," Penny said.

"I should think not!" Agatha dabbed at her lips indignantly with her napkin.

Thorne gave an irritated little snort and stood. "I must write some letters to tell people on my estates to expect me. This should take care of the ghost problem, so I will be able to leave soon."

Allison followed him.

"My lord!" Penny hastened after them. "You need to lock this up again."

She held out the necklace to him. He did not take it, but motioned her to follow him to the library, where he locked it once more in the safe.

"I wonder how they get it out," Allison said.

"I must ask you to be honest with me." Penny lifted her chin and made her tone firm. "Are the two of you playing some sort of trick on me?"

Thorne scowled. "I have better things to do with my time."

Allison reached out to Penny with both hands. "Nor would either of us be so cruel. Trust us, please! This is quite out of your experience, I know, and almost outside of my own. But it is not of our doing."

Penny nodded her head. "Then I must accept that somehow a spirit, or spirits, is involved. I wonder how they convey the necklace upstairs. It is unaccountable. You have footmen posted all night long. You would think they might see the necklace moving along, even if they don't see the ghost."

"I expect they doze a bit. Doubtless the specters use that opportunity to . . ." Thorne began to chuckle. "It would be a comic sight, wouldn't it, to see a ruby necklace floating through the air."

The two women laughed, though Penny's was a bit forced. *This is all so strange,* she thought. *I wish I could just run away from it.* But she couldn't. The Silverthornes had convinced her of their sincerity, of the reality of the situation. Thus, now that she had met and learned to like Allison, she could never abandon her while it seemed she might help her.

"I believe I will go work on my books," she announced, leaving the couple alone.

Upstairs, she took a deep breath as she looked around the studio. The easel now held the sketch pad James had purchased for her in London. The watercolors were ready. The light was perfect. What a glorious morning it was. She walked to the window and looked out over the countryside, drawing a deep breath of air.

"Ah, do not throw yourself out of the window!"

She whirled at the deep voice. "Mr. Betterton!"

"James. Please call me James."

"I thought you had gone."

"And so in despair she goes to the window, moaning at the loss of her beloved." He advanced on her, a strange lopsided grin on his face.

"No such thing! I was thinking how beautiful it is today."

"Too beautiful to be indoors. Come for a drive with me, Penelope."

"I . . ." The sound of her first name on his lips did strange things to her insides. "I don't understand why you have come back." She moved to one side and slipped past him, into the center of the room.

"The farther I went, the more miserable I felt. I have come back to make a confession."

"A confession?" She put her hand over her heart, which stuttered in her breast. He would admit that this position was made up, to assist him in breaking down her resistance to his seduction. Perhaps he would admit that the entire ghost business was made up, a hoax he perpetrated on his relatives as well as her.

"Yes. I have to confess that I adore you."

She started for the door.

"Please. Hear me out." *She looks like a deer at bay,* he thought. How foolish his sudden resolution seemed now. He had meant to stay away for a while, returning later, after Thorne had departed. The plan to court her had seemed less and less likely to succeed as he rode along. *She will still be wary of me. Why wouldn't she be? I've never given her a hint of my true feelings and intentions.* As the miles stretched between them, he felt more and more pulled to return to her and declare himself. Now his heart beat loudly, and he questioned the wisdom of his decision, but he decided he must proceed. *I am glad Allison and Thorne did not see me return. They would doubtless disapprove of my acting so precipitously.*

"I have grown very attached to you, Miss Jones. I wish you to know that I care for you deeply."

"Ah." Penny reached the door. "So deeply that you wish to offer me a slip on the shoulder, no doubt. Does your honorable cousin know of this?" She started to run, but he overtook her. Catching her by the upper arms, he restrained her, but gently.

"Not a slip on the shoulder. Never that. I have only the most honorable intentions. Please, Penelope. Listen to my suit."

"Your suit?" Her voice quavered, both at his nearness and the import of his words.

"Yes. I have fallen in love with you. I wish to marry you. There! Now you cannot have any reason to fear me." The magical change in attitude he had hoped for did not materialize.

"More reason than you know."

"I don't understand. Do you not feel anything at

all for me? Do you not think you could, if you allowed yourself to? If you stopped being so on your guard for an assault on your honor? For there will be no such assault. Never, even when I asked you to dance with me, when you were the Hartnet governess, did I have dishonorable intentions. I was drawn to you, and wished to know you better, that is all."

She lowered her head, to avoid the impact of the love light in his eyes. "James, I do like you. In fact"—boldly she threw her head back and met his eyes—"I find you very attractive. What woman would not? But I won't marry you. I wouldn't, even if I loved you very much. Especially then."

A deep line appeared between his eyebrows. "That seems an odd point of view."

"I don't believe in mixing the classes. I think that way lies misery for both parties. Certainly for the wife. And definitely for me! I could never mix in the *ton*. I would never belong, and would hate always being on the outside. And you would come to resent the way I didn't fit in, did not make you a good *ton* wife. Who knows what pain that resentment would cause both of us?"

He drew her closer. "That is nonsense. You are so intelligent, I beg leave to doubt you believe it."

"I believe it with all my heart."

"Love will overcome such minor matters as a few snobs. That is all you are really talking about here—a few ridiculous snobs." He bent his head to kiss her, and oh, how she longed for that kiss. But she turned her head away.

"No! I said *if* I loved you. I don't. And in truth, you do not know me well enough to know whether you love me or not."

It was time to regroup. James accepted that he would not accomplish his objective this day, but all must not be lost. "Then let us get to know one another better. You now know my intentions are honorable. If my return, my precipitate proposal accomplishes nothing else, I would be happy if it took down the barriers to furthering our acquaintance."

She felt sorry for him. She felt sorry for herself. But she had to crush this now, or leave.

"I am very sorry you came back. Very sorry you proposed. Especially, deeply sorry if you truly find your affections engaged. Because I can't, won't marry you! I expect I had best go away. I will find another place from which to work on the books, or else give up the idea altogether."

He put her from him, a hurt expression in his eyes. "That won't be necessary. I won't importune you. I have said what I came to say. You have nothing to fear from me."

Oh, yes, I have, she thought, tears threatening to spill from her eyes.

He moved down the hall. "Go on with your work, Miss Jones. It is important, and I will not be here to hinder you in it." Turning on his heel, he reached the stairs in three strides and quickly disappeared from view.

Taking care not to encounter his cousins, James rode away from Thorne Hall once again. At first he despaired, roundly cursing himself for this precipitous proposal. But as the miles passed, he began to feel more sanguine. She had admitted her attraction to him. He suspected that deep within, she already returned his love, though she did not wish to acknowledge this.

He must find a way to soothe her fears of being isolated among his friends. *I will suggest that Allison plan a party and invite some people we know who would be accepting of her. Her fear of being snubbed would soon be overcome.*

He whiled away the time as he rode by planning whom to invite. Allison was good friends with Lord Langley's wife, Gwynneth, who had once been a bookseller. She certainly would not snub Penelope. And his own recently acquired friend, Lord Pelham, had a sweet, friendly wife. Davida, as the daughter of a country squire, would not hold herself above Penny. And then there was Beau's wife. He doubted he could entirely cut the connection with Beauford Montrose, so why not take advantage of the fact that Lady Montrose was shy? She doubtless would welcome the opportunity to make a friend, and Penny could encourage her not to be so retiring.

An optimistic person by nature, James had almost convinced himself that success in his courtship was imminent by the time he drew near his home, Fairmont.

Penny got little work done that day. She tried and tried to concentrate, but James's hurt expression rose in her mind. The memory of his nearness, of the deep desire that had stirred in her when he tried to kiss her, made her restless. She found herself sketching him instead of friendly little frogs. At last she gave up and decided to go for a walk. Some distance from the house a small stream appeared from nowhere. A spring, perhaps. It meandered into the decorative lake. Generous random plantings of trees promised cool shade in the heat of the day. The walk would clear her mind, and the shade would rest her overheated body.

As she drew near one of the several groupings of trees around the lake, she heard giggling sounds and a deeper voice laughing. She wondered if she had happened upon a pair of servants trysting. She stopped and listened for a moment, and made out the voice of Agatha Kiesley. From there it was but a small step to guessing the owner of the other voice. Edward Bartholomew.

I thought those two were smelling of April and May! She stood irresolute in the hot sun. She had worked up quite a sweat walking, and the shade of the trees was most inviting. She had dipped her handkerchief in the tiny stream at the stone spring head along the way and discovered to her amazement that it was warm, almost hot. She then remembered James telling her, on their way into Derbyshire, that Silverthorne castle sat on top of a hot spring similar to those that had made Buxton a destination for those seeking health-giving waters. Fascinating though this was, the warm water had been a disappointment to one who was seeking a little relief from the heat.

Although Penny was far from approving assignations of any sort, she had no wish to intrude, so she began to quietly retrace her steps, when a loud, accusing voice rang out.

"So! Spying on us! I suppose that cruel Silverthorne sent you."

Penny turned around. Agatha Kiesley stood with her hands on her heart. "Oh, my dear Edward. I fear we are undone. You will be let off without a character, and I will be denied the dower house."

"Now, now, my dear. I am sure Miss Jones will not inform on us."

"Of course, she will. She is his creature. And she has disliked me from the moment she laid eyes on me."

Penny had to bite her tongue to keep from replying waspishly that she rather thought the shoe was on the other foot. Instead she recited to herself the verse from the Bible about doing good to those who spitefully use you.

"I will not give you away, Miss Kiesley, but I do not think that this sort of assignation is in the best interests of either you or Mr. Bartholomew."

"Did you hear her, my dear? She will say nothing," Mr. Bartholomew said.

"How dare she set herself up as my judge, my preceptor in behavior? You go above yourself, Miss Jones."

Penny yearned to ask Mr. Bartholomew what he saw in this harpy, but she kept quiet. After another few moments of fussing on Agatha's part, and soothing on Bartholomew's, the latter left them, saying it would be best if he and Agatha were not seen leaving together.

Penny shook her head. "I should think you would have thought of that before coming here," she blurted out. "Anyone walking that path can be seen from almost any room on the west side of the hall."

Agatha put her head in her hands and began to cry. "It is true. It is so true. We must never meet again, my love. I have known for a very long time that I put your employment at risk by doing so. Leave me now." She turned away from him and held out her hand in a dramatic gesture that would have suited a Cheltenham tragedy. Bartholomew took it and kissed it fervently, then hastened past Penny.

Do not leave me here with her, Penny wanted to cry out. The two women stood awkwardly confronting each other in silence.

"I must get out of the sun," Penny said, moving gingerly past the older woman and into the shade of the trees. She spotted a bench facing the lake, and sat down.

"You really won't say anything to Silverthorne?"

Penny looked up. "No, I won't. But why are you so afraid of him? He is a kind man. Surely, he would—."

"Kind! You do not know him. He would discharge Mr. Bartholomew merely to spite me."

"If he objected, would you still marry Mr. Bartholomew?"

Agatha sighed and looked out over the lake. "Yes. I know he is not of my class, but I am tired of being lonely and unloved. He is a refined man, a gentleman in the true sense of the word, though of no independent means. Where is the harm? I have even asked him to share my small income so that we could leave here and marry. But he will not. He is too proud. He insists he must be able to provide for me."

Penny nodded, and patted the seat beside her. "I hope you may find a way to be together. I assure you once again I will say nothing."

Agatha sat down heavily. "Thank you. I thought you might understand, having set your cap for one above you as you have."

"What ever do you mean?"

"Well, it is plain to see you hope to attach Mr.

Betterton. But I do not think it will happen. He is a confirmed bachelor, I fear. He has given up some of his worst habits, or so Allison tells me. But then, dear Allison is so easily imposed upon. Still, he is said to be much improved, yet he has not married though he has claimed for the past three years to be looking for a bride. How hard can it be, with so much money—and passable looks, too?"

Passable? Penny thought of the way his dark hair curled over his high forehead, the way his brows and lips quirked when he smiled, the slight Roman cast to his nose, the firm lips and chin.

"Very attractive, I should call him," she could not keep herself from saying.

"Ah, dear. I do hope you have not given your heart to that rogue, for he will trample on it, I fear."

Agatha smiled in a sickening way that told Penny the woman was trying her best to upset her. *If only I could tell her he has just proposed to me, and wipe that smirk off her face.* But she could not do that. She hadn't the least idea of confiding in this spiteful woman under any circumstances, and especially not about James. She could not say whether the Silverthornes would support his interest in her or be appalled by it, but either way would be most uncomfortable for her, and perhaps for Mr. Betterton.

So she held her peace, and finally Agatha stood up and walked away.

Chapter Twelve

"That ghost was in our room again last night, scolding Allison." Thus did Thorne greet Penny the next day.

"I am so sorry. Did you get any sleep?" Penny studied Allison's face for signs of exhaustion.

"Yes. When she started in, I got my pad and wrote it down as best I could. She seemed pleased by this and repeated her message slowly so I could get it right. I have it here."

She handed a tablet to Penny, who sat down and absently sipped on a cup of tea a servant put in front of her as she began deciphering the message.

"What does it mean?" Allison asked.

"Much as before. It says the necklace is not yours, that it and the rest of the treasure belong to the daughter of Lady Winifred."

"Ah." Thorne frowned. "Does she say anything else?"

"I can't make it out. Something about the castle." Penny muttered the syllables under her breath, trying to make them sound like something in Welsh.

"Not that castle again," Agatha groaned.

Penny looked up. The three were following her every word.

"Then?" Thorne leaned forward impatiently.

"She said this to me two nights ago. It was part of why I was afraid to go to the castle."

"What does she say?"

"If am deciphering this correctly, she says the daughter of Lady Winifred must go to Silverthorne Castle. I'm not that person. Still, if we are somehow related . . ." Penny shrugged her shoulders. "But I went. So what more does she want of me? She must be referring to someone else."

The others had no answer.

"Perhaps the rest of the treasure means the missing stones in the necklace," Allison mused. "After we break our fast, let us examine it more closely.

Penny teased the necklace into shape and studied the pattern. "I make out the missing piece to include three small rubies and a pair of diamonds. Plus the chain, of course."

"Dratted spirits. I had best delay my trip. I don't intend to leave until this ghost is laid," Thorne said.

"Hmmm. Penny, are you willing to go to the castle today and look around for them? I will accompany you," Allison offered.

"Will you let them go there and share your father's and my beloved nephew's fate?" Agatha shrieked at Thorne.

"I will not let them go into any area of danger. If that ghost wants Penny to have those other jewels, it will have to bring them to a safe place. I will go with you, of course."

Penny's head throbbed with tension. She disliked the idea of going to the castle, and dreaded any further interactions with the ghosts. But she owed it to Allison to do her best.

Thorne stood and told Penny to pick up the necklace and follow him. She thought he would put it back in the safe, but he didn't. He went into the drawing room, followed by Penny, Allison, and of course Agatha. He announced loudly to the room at large, "I believe that this necklace belongs to Miss Penelope Jones, and hereby transfer ownership to her."

"But . . ." Both Penny and Agatha started to object, but Thorne held up his hand. "I feel that this is what needs to be done," he announced firmly.

"Come along." He went into the study and repeated the same words. Then he led the trio of women upstairs and into his and Allison's quarters. In each room he made the same announcement, and then they went to Penny's room, where he announced it again.

"There. Perhaps they will leave my wife alone now."

"But I cannot leave such a valuable object in my room," Penny protested.

"Ask me to lock it in the safe for you." Thorne nodded his head and looked around the room meaningfully. So Penny spoke the words loudly, first in English, then in Welch.

"I accept this necklace from Lord Silverthorne, and ask him to lock it in his safe, where it will not be stolen from me."

Thorne motioned her to follow him, leading her back into his quarters. "Again," he commanded.

So she loudly repeated the words. Then they went downstairs, and he had her repeat them in the drawing room and study. There he opened his safe, and Penny put the jewels in the box he had originally presented them in.

"Now," he said, "perhaps that will be the end of the hauntings, especially if we can retrieve the missing piece of the necklace. I don't want to leave on my annual visit to my estates until I know that Allison will be left alone to get her rest at night."

"I hope it may be so." Penny's mind was whirling. This necklace—this gorgeous object for which, if she was not mistaken, several people had died—was to be hers? And if so, what would she do with it? She felt an odd connection to it. The thought of disposing of it gave a sharp tug on her heartstrings. Yet for such as her to own something so valuable was foolish beyond permission, especially since selling it would allow her to help her family so much.

A dowry for Mary! College for Thomas! Her mind began ticking off delightful possibilities.

Penny, Allison, and Thorne went to the castle afterward, leaving Agatha at home, for she never would set foot anywhere near the place. They searched the grounds, to no avail. Then Thorne had one of the workmen closely inspect the place where the skeleton had been found.

The worker lifted several rocks from the area, examining nooks and crannies, where stray pieces of jewelry might have landed. After a few minutes he gave a whoop and called out, "I have it."

He clambered off the rock pile and climbed the sturdy wooden stairs that had been installed for the workmen to ascend and descend into the debris field.

"Be this what you was a-hoping fer, my lord?"

he asked, holding up a section of gold chain with three rubies and two diamonds. It was easy to see that the pattern would fit exactly into the necklace. The chain had been badly flattened, but the jewels themselves were as remarkably undamaged as the rest of the necklace.

"It is, indeed." Thorne reached into his pocket and handed the man a small purse of coins.

"I pay them for any valuable discoveries. They are searched each evening for contraband, and fired if any is found. Prosecution for theft is threatened if they return to the site. The reward plus the fear of punishment seems to work fairly well. We have recovered quite a variety of artifacts."

Penny nodded, her mind mostly focused on the string of jewels in her hand. She could no longer doubt that her dreams were linked to the ghosts. Her mind opened to the possibility, and she began wondering about the woman little Jason had seen across the cliff.

"Could we return by the other road, sir? I would like to get out and . . . look at the castle from that angle."

Thorne nodded. Allison looked into her face and then hugged her. "I know how awesome and unsettling this is," she whispered into Penny's ear.

When they reached the place where Jason had said the lady beckoned to them, Penny got down and walked slowly, cautiously to the cliff's edge, and made herself look fully at the castle. Then she narrowed her eyes, trying to shut out the modern repairs.

Unsuccessful. She closed her eyes, and suddenly the castle was complete. A white handkerchief waved from the windows. Men fought for their lives on the battlements. Penny shook her head. "I don't want to see it," she murmured.

"Then turn around. Turn to me, daughter." She turned, and slowly opened her eyes. The Silverthornes had disappeared. The terrain seemed different, too. The ground was scorched and torn up, and a pair of abandoned cannons stood nearby. A beautiful woman in a shabby cloak stood in front of her, holding out her arms.

"You have the look of her, even." The woman smiled.

"The look of . . . ?"

"Of my darling Charlotte. Named, of course, for her father. Oh, how I wish I'd been able to give her her dowry. She wouldn't have had to marry a nobody like Iltry, if she had possessed my fortune in jewels."

"You have something of the look of my mother, too. But I do not understand. Why did you not tell Charlotte of the jewels?"

"The owner of the castle in her lifetime was not one to part with what he would have seen as his property. At any rate, we could not communicate with Charlotte. Her mind was closed to us." Lady Winifred's face reflected an ancient sorrow.

Penny murmured soothingly to her. "It is all very sad. To think you have lingered here so many years! Your daughter had children. There have been many heirs through the years. Why not give the jewels to them?"

"We had to wait until the conditions were right. An owner of the castle who would do the right thing. Someone who could hear us, at least in her dreams. And a less numerous progeny." Lady Winifred smiled wryly. "Split so many ways, what good would this treasure have done? I have waited until there was only one. You shall have a dowry. You shall marry well. So it should have been for my Charlotte. So it shall be for you."

"Why does the maid linger? And the soldier who killed you?"

"Owain? He did not kill me. In his grief, he started to, but I pleaded for my life. Then we were attacked. He died trying to save me. All for naught. I, too, fought with my attackers." She extracted from the folds of her dress a small but wicked-looking sword. "But in vain. As I retreated from their swords, I plunged down the cliff to my death. The jewels in my cap are still there, behind a ledge, waiting for you along with my bones. You will give me a Christian burial?"

"Of course. But still, why do the servants linger? Such devotion . . ."

"Not devotion, alas. Guilt. You see, Bronwyn and Owain set out to steal my fortune, under the guise of helping me escape the man who had forced me to agree to marry him. It resulted in her death and, in a sense, Owain's, for he lingered when she was captured, when he might have escaped, and was slain himself. We found ourselves bound to this world by our ambitions, our sins, our desire for a resolution. Once the fortune is delivered into your hands, we can all go to our rest. You will persist, will you not? You must go to the castle at the dark of the moon."

"The dark . . . Oh, dear."

"You might be able to see us in the dark. It is very tiring to manifest when there is any light. Whether you can see us or not, we will bring the treasure to you there. You hesitate. You do not like the castle, I know, but it is taxing upon our powers to move physical objects, and we need you to be as close to their resting place as possible."

Cold. I am so cold. Penny could not answer.

"I see you are afraid. Not unwise, actually, for there is danger lurking. There is one who would take away your treasure if he can. You and your cavalier will face this danger together. Then you will have a fortune. You will feel no obligation to marry him. You may marry where you will. But if you marry him, I will give you my blessing."

"You speak of Mr. Betterton?" *I can never marry him,* she warned her suddenly hopeful heart.

"The child calls him Uncle James?"

"Yes. James Betterton."

"You will be his equal, my love. Equal to almost any in the land. You are descended from a king. I was the daughter of an earl. You will have a fortune in jewels, and perhaps the Iltry estate, if your country's laws can be satisfied. You may look very high for a husband."

The radiant look on Lady Winifred's face as she predicted this future caused Penny to hold back speaking of her reservations. She found she yearned to go into the woman's outstretched arms, but when she approached, she felt a bone-deep chill. A look of sorrow came over Lady Winifred's face, and she backed away, holding a hand up in warning. She began to fade from sight.

"Penny. Penny. Wake up. Oh, dear. Thorne, she is so cold." Allison's concerned voice reached her faintly, as if from far away.

Penny tried to open her eyes, but couldn't. She felt something warm enveloping her, felt herself being lifted up. She forced her eyes open at last, just as Thorne began to struggle to put her on the wagon's second seat.

"I am all right. Let me. I can sit up."

"Oh, thank goodness." Allison's voice still seemed to come from far away. Penny managed the strength to help Thorne seat her in the wagon. Allison quickly joined her and threw her arms around her to steady her.

Chapter Thirteen

$\mathcal{P}$enny learned from the Silverthornes that she had slumped to the ground in a deep trance shortly after leaving the carriage. She told them as much as she could remember of the experience.

"Drat! I had hoped we were through with this ghost business." Thorne stalked to the window that looked out from Penny's bedroom over the pastoral scene beyond. "I need to get on with my trip so I can be back here well before time for the baby to be born."

"You don't need to stay on my account," Penny protested from deep beneath the covers. She couldn't seem to get warm, even with hot water bottles tucked beside her.

"No, of course you needn't stay," Allison said. "Lady Winifred said Penny could take James to protect her." Husband and wife exchanged a long glance, which seemed to convey some secret, but Penny couldn't fathom what. She was too distracted by the way her heart sped up at the mention of James's name.

She was deeply torn by this suggestion. On the one hand, the ghost had suggested she could bring James along; she had said no such thing of Thorne.

On the other, she recognized by the erratic motion of her heart that she was in danger of losing it to James Betterton. She tried to harden her heart. Nothing would change if she had the treasure, really. Even with a fortune, she would never be accepted in the *ton*. Both she and James, and possibly their children, would suffer for the mésalliance. She would never risk marrying when the marriage was doomed from the start.

Still, she felt it would be churlish to keep Thorne from his necessary travels. The idea of going to the castle at the dark of the moon alarmed her very much, but she found that if she must do so, James Betterton appealed to her much more as a companion.

"I'd have to have a maid go along. Do you think that would serve to protect my reputation?"

"Absolutely. We'll ask your personal maid. I'm sure for a few guineas, she'd gladly go. In fact, she has expressed herself as jealous of Marie for being able to see ghosts, so she is not in the least hysterical." Allison smiled and put a soothing hand on Penny's brow. "You rest the remainder of the day, my dear, and we'll discuss this more tonight."

Since sleep seemed to be tugging at her eyelids, Penny nodded her head, closed her eyes, and almost immediately drifted off.

"Another treasure? Is there no end of what this chit will seek to steal? And I do not think a hey-go-mad little miss such as Jane will be a proper chaperon, though I doubt you desire much in the way of chaperonage, Miss Jones. Likely have your eye on marrying into the family as well as taking away from it a fortune in jewels."

Penny never ceased to be astonished at the amount of venom in Agatha Kiesley, aimed at almost anyone except Allison. She sighed and folded her hands in her lap, lowering her eyes demurely.

"I fear you are right about the chaperonage. I need an older woman. A woman of impeccable character. Of course, Allison has no business being up there at night in her condition. I was hoping perhaps *you* would consider accompanying me, Miss Kiesley. Not that I think Mr. Betterton would do me any harm. Strictly for appearance's sake, though."

Agatha's eyes goggled at this suggestion. "Insane. Quite, quite insane, to imagine I would involve myself in your plan to fleece my relative. Most particularly by going up to that castle that was the death of my dear little nephew? No! Never!"

"Ah, well. I am sorry, ma'am. I had such hopes of you."

Allison slid a sideward glance at Penny and put her handkerchief up to her mouth to smother a grin. Thorne coughed into his cupped hand.

"I am relieved to hear you refuse," Mr. Bartholomew said, his eyes on Agatha. "I cannot like the idea of a delicate, gently bred female exposing herself to such a situation."

Agatha blushed and preened herself. "I am glad *someone* cares what happens to me. That is, to Miss Jones and myself, for Thorne cannot be trusted to look after us."

Just then the door to the drawing room opened. The Silverthorne butler announced, "Mr. James Betterton, Sir Beauford Montrose, and Lady Montrose."

Thorne helped Allison to her feet, and she hastened to greet her new guests. Once they were seated, she told James, "I sent for you just this afternoon, but surely you had not received that summons yet?"

"No." James glanced at Penny, a strange look on his face. "Sir Beauford was on his way here. He stopped by Fairmont to rest his cattle, and found me in residence. When I heard his mission, I thought it best to accompany him."

"On his way here?" Allison's amazement showed in her voice. Sir Beauford was one of James's friends from his rakehell days. She had never approved of the man, though he seemed to have settled down a little since marrying his wife, a short, pretty brunette.

"Yes, Lady Silverthorne. I felt it my duty to come here and tell you and Lord Silverthorne that you were about to be imposed upon by a clever little schemer."

"There, didn't I say so?" Agatha snapped.

A sound passed Lady Montrose's lips, something between a gasp and a sigh. She sat looking down at her hands in a gesture oddly reminiscent of Penny's of a few minutes before. There was no humor in her expression, however. Her pallor suggested someone near to fainting.

All eyes turned for a moment to Penny. She was almost as pale as Lady Montrose, but her chin was up and her eyes firmly fixed on Sir Beauford's face.

"I think you had best explain yourself, Sir Beauford," Thorne growled.

"According to the papers, a valuable ruby-and-diamond necklace has been found on your property, and claimed by Miss Penelope Jones, here. Is that true?"

"A necklace has been found," Thorne agreed.

"And claimed by that impostor. I knew she—"

"Enough!" James shouted at Agatha. "Let Miss Jones answer to the charges."

"Charges?" Penny turned her eyes on him.

"I mean . . . No, I don't mean charges. But Sir Beauford has told me something unexpected, something that I hope you can explain."

"I would like to remind all of you that I never laid claim to that necklace. But what business it is of Sir Beauford's whether I have it or not, I cannot make out."

"The paper said it was an inheritance through your mother's line," Sir Beauford said, eyes darting from Penny to Thorne.

She stared at him, unblinking. "The paper said so, on the basis of partial information. But I still insist that you say on what basis *you* thrust yourself into the situation?"

Sir Beauford jumped up from his chair, hands clenched. "You know very well what business it is of mine. If it is an inheritance through your mother's line, wouldn't it go to the oldest daughter?"

"Your point being?"

"I ought to slap that smug face of yours," Sir Beauford said. He started toward her, only to be brought up short by a firm clasp on his sleeve by James.

Her expression softening a little, Penny looked at Lady Montrose. "You must explain yourself, Sir Beauford, before we can make any progress at all."

"You know very well that my wife is your older sister. That is the explanation."

"I did not know if I could claim her as my sister

or not. You forbade me to do so some time back, if you will recall," Penny said.

"This is the sister you 'lost,' isn't it?" James asked.

"So your wife is now my sister, Sir Beauford?"

"Yes, yes, yes! There! Now let's have that necklace."

"Wait a minute." Agatha's nose seemed to quiver like that of a dog on the scent of a fox. "Your wife is the illegitimate daughter of a nobleman, isn't she? That is the tale as I heard it."

"You mean your mother . . ." Allison looked pityingly at Penny.

"I won't allow you to besmirch my mother's reputation, Sir Beauford."

"But you won't deny you are sisters?" He looked at her assessingly.

Penny crossed to where Lady Montrose sat almost shrinking into the sofa. She sat down beside her and put her hand over the other woman's hands. Instantly they intertwined with hers, as if Lady Montrose were holding on to a lifeline. "I would never deny my sister. You had best revise your account, however, if you have any hope at all of achieving your goal." She lifted her eyes and looked directly at Sir Beauford in a challenging manner.

He paused a moment, seeming unsure of himself.

"So which is the lie, and which the true," James hissed. "I thought marriage had improved you, Sir Beauford, but you're still your old, opportunistic self."

"None of it is a lie. At least, about them being sisters. Thing is, Miss Jones comes from a large, clambering family. Mushrooms, every one. Except for my beloved Susan. She was ashamed to be related to them."

Lady Montrose began to cry softly.

"Dear little creature wanted to spare me from being embarrassed and put upon by her family, so we made up that business about her illegitimacy. Thought saying her father was a nobleman who wished to remain anonymous would ease her way in society, too."

"And yours." James's contemptuous sneer spurred his friend into a spirited defense.

"You can't know what it is like, to love someone so far beneath you. You want to protect her, make her able to move about in society. It was a harmless fib. And now her sister uses it to cheat her out of an inheritance."

Penny did not deny any of this. Instead, she rose, tugging on Lady Montrose's hands. "I thank you for giving me back my sister, Sir Beauford. She is worth more to me than a dozen necklaces. I beg the rest of you will excuse us while we have a little reunion."

"As if I would let my pure little wife associate with such an amoral—"

"You cannot have it both ways, Sir Beauford. She is my sister, or the necklace is mine."

Sir Beauford turned his wife toward him. "Do you wish to be private with your sister, my dear?"

"Of course she does." Penny did not allow the cringing Lady Montrose to answer, but almost dragged her from the room.

"Well! I never!" Agatha exclaimed.

"Oh, if you knew that family as I do, you would

not be surprised at her encroaching ways. I suppose she has talked herself into a nice position here, convinced you she was the only daughter of that woman, and so forth."

Allison looked at her husband, then at James. "I never saw anything encroaching about her."

"And it's true as true that she never claimed that necklace," James said. Beau's words stung him. *You can't know what it is like, to love someone so far beneath you. You want to protect her, make her able to move about in society.* James's mind raced as he remembered Penny's refusal to consider marriage to him. Surely it was this connection, and Sir Beauford's reaction to marriage to one beneath himself socially, that had formed Penny's notions about marriage into the *ton*. No wonder she had refused his proposal.

Agatha interrupted his attempts to make sense of the situation with her strident voice. "She never claimed it in so many words, perhaps, but she did not refuse it when Lord Silverthorne gave it to her."

"Then it is hers to dispose of?" Sir Beauford's avaricious smile curled his lips unpleasantly.

Thorne rocked back and forth on his heels a second. "I don't know. That is up to Miss Jones. And the ghosts, of course."

"Ghosts?" Disdain laced Sir Beauford's tone. "Oh, that is right. You and your wife have experience with that sort of thing. Well, I expect Miss Penelope Jones has managed to use that to her advantage, pretending to see these ghosts, to attempt to make off with that necklace before the true heiress arrives."

Thorne and Allison exchanged glances. "Actually," Allison said, "it is I who have seen the ghosts."

"Been driven half mad by them, too," Agatha said, glaring at Thorne with her "everything is your fault" look.

"It is obvious that you dined some while ago," Thorne said. "I'll have a cold collation brought to you here."

He went out the door, as if to summon the butler himself. In truth, he hoped for a word with Penny and Lady Montrose. A footman told him they had gone into the library. He peeked in and found the two locked in an embrace, both women crying.

It being his policy to avoid crying women where possible, he returned to the drawing room after ordering that cold collation.

"I will have something sent to your wife and Miss Jones. I am told they are having a tearful reunion."

"I dislike that scheming female making my wife cry." Sir Beauford started for the door.

James stood up abruptly. "I say, Beau. Thorne has the most fantastic brandy. Best French stuff. All duties paid, too, though as I recall, you never let such considerations stop you from enjoying a glass of fine liquor."

He threw an arm around Sir Beauford, affecting great bonhomie, and irresistibly drew the man to the liquor cabinet. Thorne obligingly opened it and invited them to drink up.

"Well!" Agatha sniffed and stood. "Bad enough you drink yourself into a stupor after dinner. To start it up again in the drawing room . . ."

"Aunt Agatha, perhaps you should turn in," Allison suggested. "This looks to be a long night."

"A very good idea." Mr. Bartholomew stood and offered Agatha his hand. "You may hear something not fit for delicate ears."

Agatha appeared torn between curiosity and the desire to seem as delicate as her admirer thought her to be. She took Bartholomew's hand and stood, but could not resist a parting shot before exiting the room.

"Sir Beauford, before I go, I want to thank you for exposing this little Welsh schemer. Do be sure that the rest of the treasure is recovered before you leave."

"The rest of the treasure?" Sir Beauford was instantly distracted from the brandy. "There's more?"

"A great deal more, if what she told us is true." Agatha looked at the disgusted faces of Thorne, James, and Allison. She addressed herself, somewhat apologetically, to Allison. "I am sorry, dear. You have been deceived and imposed upon. You really would not want to be a party to giving this treasure to the wrong person, though, would you? I know your conscience would not accept that." She patted Allison's cheek.

Allison pulled away and answered through clenched teeth, "No, Aunt Agatha, I certainly would not. In fact, I positively won't allow it."

Sir Beauford looked at her in some alarm. "See here. I can prove my claim."

"Since so far any hints as to the owner of the treasure have come from ghosts, that may be difficult," Thorne said. "But don't let me keep you from sampling my brandy. And here is the cold collation."

Chapter Fourteen

Penny dragged Susan into the library. She let go of her sister's hand when they reached the center of the room and turned to face her.

"Penny. Oh, Penny, I am so sorry. He has no right to do this to you. You have so little. This is your chance to have a dowry and make a good marriage."

Penny let out her breath with a whoosh. "I knew it. You aren't a willing participant in this charade."

"No. Oh, no! But when he wants something . . ." Susan shuddered.

"I know. I know." Penny studied her sister's woeful face. "He made you write Papa that last letter."

"Oh, how often I have wept over that awful letter, telling him I was ashamed of my family, and did not wish to hear from any of you anymore. It was so untrue."

Penny opened her arms, and Susan rushed into them. Both women were sobbing. It was thus that Thorne found them, briefly peeking in the room and then hastily withdrawing. Unaware of his quick surveillance, Penny at last regained command of herself and drew Susan over to one of the library tables, where they seated themselves side by side.

"How does he treat you?"

Susan's shoulders shook. "When he is angry, he becomes very violent. He owes a great deal of money and is quite desperate. You see, my father will quit giving him money for keeping his secret. His wife passed away recently, you see. Once she was gone, he no longer had to fear hurting her feelings with knowledge of his long-ago affair. He offered Montrose a sum to allow me to go live with him as his acknowledged daughter, but my dear husband said it was not high enough. He thinks to extract more from him by abusing me."

Penny shuddered at this cruelty. "He has been blackmailing your father?"

"Yes. Oh, Penny, our whole marriage has been a lie. I know my father meant it for the best, but it wasn't love at first sight, as I had thought. My father told Montrose about me, deliberately sent him to the academy to 'accidentally' meet me. He had promised Montrose a large sum of money as my dowry if he could win my affection. And he did. But he never had any affection for me. Only for money! I learned that when I confronted him about infidelities."

This brought on another flood of tears, which Penny had to soothe. She could only imagine the heartache of being in love and finding that the love was not returned.

"So when he saw the article in the paper, he decided to come here and claim the necklace, gambling that I wouldn't betray you or refuse you?" Penny asked.

"Yes. I begged him not to. I won't let you give up your necklace! I'll let him beat me. It is just . . . I am a coward, Penny."

"No, you are not. Don't blame yourself for his cruelty."

"All I've ever done for you is hurt you."

"Nonsense. It was *your* father who paid for my tuition at the academy, at your request. And didn't you help get me my position with Lady Hartnet after that unfortunate incident ended my first employment?"

"But I didn't do enough. You were always so kind to me. So utterly accepting of the bastard Papa Jones adopted to help my parents keep their secret."

"I loved you, and love you still, as much as if you were my blood sister. Would you like to leave Montrose, Susan?" Penny tilted Susan's head up and forced her to meet her eyes.

Susan's lips trembled. "Yes," she whispered. "But he would never agree to it."

"What if I had a great deal more to offer him than the necklace? Thousands of dollars' worth of jewels?"

At this offer, a candlestick rose off the table several inches, then slammed down. Susan jumped back in terror. "Are there dark forces at work here, Penny?"

Penny shook her head, projecting greater certainty than she really felt. "Some rather single-minded ghosts, is all. Listen, Owain. Lift the candlestick up gently if you hear me and understand my words."

Slowly the stick rose about two inches off the table.

"Lady Winifred told me what happened with the necklace and the other treasure. You stole from her, you and your sweetheart Bronwyn. Did you not?"

The stick wavered, as if the hand that held it trembled.

"You both regret it, I know. You wish to give these items to their rightful owner. But once you give them to me, they are mine to do with as I please. Aren't they? After all, to realize their value, I would have to part with them anyway. I would have to sell them. Set the stick down, now. I am going to the castle tonight, and you and Bronwyn are going to bring the rest of Lady Winifred's treasure to me. Agreed?"

Once again, the candlestick rose slowly off the table, then returned.

"Good. Thank you. You are a faithful servant."

Penny turned to Susan, whose eyes were wide in her pale face. "There is nothing to fear. I am going to draw up a document. If Sir Beauford wants to have my valuables, he is going to have to give me something valuable in return: my sister's freedom."

Susan launched herself forward, into Penny's arms. "I'll never forget this! Never. If I ever have the chance to repay you, I will."

"I know." Penny stroked her hair. "Oh, Susan. Will you go live with Papa, perhaps? Or would the lure of society be too great?"

"It would be heaven to be back in that crowded parsonage full of love and laughter," Susan said. "But my father will be all alone now. If he wants me, I will go to him."

"Very well, give me a few minutes to work on this document."

* * *

While Penny wrote out the document, a servant brought a tray with food and tea. Susan munched daintily on a sandwich while answering Penny's questions about Sir Beauford's character and what secrets would be likely to make him keep the agreement once he had spent the money he made selling the jewels. Neither woman trusted him to keep his word without some threat hanging over his head.

When she was satisfied with what she had written, she made a fair copy. Susan, looking at the draft with her, made another copy.

When they had finished, Penny stepped to the library door and called to a waiting footman, "Would you ask Sir Beauford to come here?"

To her surprise, Sir Beauford seemed considerably well-to-go when he arrived, though he comprehended the document she presented him sufficiently to begin swearing loudly.

"Come, Montrose. You never loved me," Susan coaxed. "Unless you change your ways and begin to live within your means, you won't even have a way to support me soon. Let us separate."

"Why should I care to keep you? But I have no heir. You have given me only a puny daughter, who died. You are a failure."

Susan sighed. "I know. Which is why we should separate. It is unlikely there will be an heir, and if there were, an heir to what? You have lost your land, my dowry, every other penny you could get your hands on. You will game away any money you gain from this extortion, too. It is a sickness with you. So you will not be able to support a wife, much less a child."

Not liking this frank assessment, Sir Beauford raised his fist to her, but for once she did not cringe, and after a moment he lowered it.

"There are really ghosts?" He looked at Penny dubiously.

"Yes. And tonight I am going to receive the rest of my inheritance. I will turn it over to you in exchange for Susan's freedom. You will never attempt to reclaim her—do you understand? If you do, I will make this information public and you will not be able to hold your head up in society. Cheating at cards, I am told, is regarded as particularly unforgiveable in the *ton*."

"Oh, very well. Give it to me. I'll sign."

"One minute. We must have a witness. Susan, ask the footman to summon Mr. Betterton."

"No! If he reads this, my secrets will be out."

"Not at all. He will sign it without reading it." Penny had already selected a book of the perfect size. She slipped the two copies of the documents into the book so that the date showed at the tops, and the bottoms protruded out just enough to allow for signatures.

When James walked in, Penny turned to him, dreading to see disgust in his eyes, and saw only concern. She explained to him that he was to sign as witness both copies of the document, without reading them.

She slid the papers back and forth enough to make clear that the dated tops, which he could see, were part of the papers that required signing. James looked carefully at Susan, Penny, and Sir Beauford.

"Will I ever know what this document says?"

"Only if one of the parties does not keep his or

her word." So saying, Penny signed her full name
with a flourish. She stepped aside so that Susan
could sign with a trembling hand. Finally Sir Beauford signed, and James witnessed their signatures.

"You should have another witness," he said.

"No, this will be enough. My word is my bond,
after all." Sir Beauford glared at Penny. "Not
something a woman could grasp, eh, James, honor
and all that?"

James made a little huffing sound, not returning
Sir Beauford's smile.

Penny raised an admonitory finger. "You keep
to your end of the bargain, starting now. That
means no more slander of me or my sister." Montrose sneered, but kept his mouth shut.

She folded the two copies separately, and sealed
them with wax and a seal from the library's desk.
"Mr. Betterton, would you keep one copy of this
document, please? And I have to ask you to say
nothing of this to Lord and Lady Silverthorne."
She raised pleading eyes to his. "I know how much
you will dislike keeping secrets from them. I hate
to ask."

He nodded. "I will not speak of it unless forced
to do so by misbehavior on the part of one of the
parties." He looked squarely at Montrose as he
said this.

"It seems you have a champion, Penny," Montrose sneered.

She smiled, looking up at James. "Yes. It seems
that I do. We had best return to the drawing
room."

Susan scuttled out of the room without looking
at her husband, who motioned for Penny to pre-

cede him. She shook her head. "I need a brief word with Mr. Betterton."

He glared at her. "You'd best be careful what you say."

She nodded her assent. He shrugged and left the room with an unsteady gait.

Penny turned to face James. "Mr. Betterton, while you were away, some interesting information has come to light."

"You mean your encounter with Lady Winifred? Yes, the others were telling me about it just now."

"Are you willing to go up to the castle with me tonight?" At his nod, she went on. "I have another favor to ask you. I know I have no right to impose on you in this way, but . . ."

"I am at your service." James had felt thrilled that Penny had trusted him enough to ask him to take her to the castle at night, and now he basked in the warmth in her eyes as she looked up at him.

"I know I can trust your discretion in this matter. I would like you to put that document away, but if ever I ask you to, or if either my sister or I should die under suspicious circumstances, please open it. I will leave it to you to decide what action to take, if any."

"I will do as you ask."

She put her hand out to shake his, sealing their bargain. He held on to her hand, looking deep into her eyes. "Penny, I wish you could trust me enough to confide in me. I might be able to help you some other way than by giving your inheritance away."

"How did you . . . ? Oh, I suppose it must be obvious. I thank you for assuming that it is mine to give away, rather than that I was trying to steal it."

"I could never believe that of you."

Penny knew she should pull her hand away, knew she should step away herself, but she couldn't make herself do it. Rather, she felt herself drawn even closer to him.

"Thank you for that. That document binds Susan and me, as well as Sir Beauford. It prevents me from responding to clarify the situation in any way. Tonight I hope that we can retrieve the treasure. Once it is in the hands of my sister . . ."

"She really is your sister?"

"Please do not ask me any more."

"Very well." He brought her hand to his lips and kissed it tenderly. She felt herself trembling deep inside. Abruptly she jerked her hand free and moved away from him.

"My sister and I will be visiting our family in Wales soon. Then I will look for another position. I am sure the Silverthornes will no longer wish to have dealings with a woman who tried to cheat her sister out of her inheritance. We had best get back to the drawing room."

James watched her go, saddened by the return of the frost maiden who had seemed to be thawing toward him. *Sir Beauford always was a bit of a rum touch. I may not know precisely what this document says, but I can guess what is going on.* He wished somehow he could help Penny and her sister, but knowing the absolute control husbands had over their wives, he doubted he could do so without challenging Sir Beauford to a duel. And what excuse, exactly, did he have for that?

Penny linked arms with her sister and swept into the drawing room with a smile on her face. "We have healed the breach between us entirely," she told the Silverthornes. "I regret that I did not tell of her existence before, but if you will recall, I barely believed in the ghosts, and did not know how to deal with the situation. Revealing that she was my sister would have revealed that she was not, as Sir Beauford had given out, the daughter of a nobleman. I realize I have no right to claim your confidence, but I always intended to see that the jewels went to their rightful owner."

Lord Silverthorne, who had been in quiet discussion with his wife when Penny and the other three returned to the drawing room, stood and bowed respectfully. "We do not mistrust you at all, do we, my love?" He looked down at his wife, who nodded her head.

"It seems, then, that the necklace may belong to Lady Montrose. Sir Beauford, there is one thing you must understand. This necklace, and any other treasure found, will be Miss Jones's, or your wife's, only if I agree to it. They will remain in my possession until I am quite satisfied that the ghosts will not return to annoy my wife."

Sir Beauford did not look pleased by this, and began to sputter something about his rights.

Thorne stepped up to the man, confronting him nose to nose. "There are no rights here but mine, and they are based on possession. There is no documentary proof that the items found in the rubble from the castle belong to anyone else. It is only a surmise we have arrived at based on the behavior of the ghosts. You would be very hard pressed to bring ghosts into court to plead your case."

Sir Beauford turned to Penny, who could only shrug her shoulders as if to say, "I told you so."

"Very well. It is understood."

"In that case, I will go get the necklace out of the safe. It will declare its true owner."

Sir Beauford sneered. "What? Does it talk?"

"In a manner of speaking, yes."

Penny sat tensely on the edge of her chair, knowing Lord Silverthorne had every intention of testing Susan's ability to hold the necklace without having her hand frozen. As soon as he entered the room, she stood and intercepted him.

"Do you mind if I look at it one last time before giving it to my sister?"

Thorne lifted a skeptical eyebrow, but after a moment's hesitation he held out the open box, and she lifted out the cascade of rubies and diamonds, gently shaping them as she did so.

She could hear Susan's indrawn breath and Sir Beauford's low but audible exclamation at the sight. With a surprising pang of sadness in her heart, she held the necklace out to Susan. "Take it, sister. It is yours."

Susan, after hesitating for a moment, eyes fixed on Penny's, reached out for it. "Oh, it is so lovely. What workmanship! I did not know they made anything so elaborate or fine in the seventeenth century."

To Penny's enormous relief, Susan showed no discomfort while handling the necklace. She had succeeded in convincing its ghostly protectors that she had the right to give it away.

"Let me put it on you, my dear," Sir Beauford purred, lifting it from his wife's hands. Without incident he affixed the necklace to Susan's neck. He turned her so that she could see in a mirror. "Lovely, indeed."

Tears flowed down Susan's cheeks. "Oh, Montrose . . ."

"I know. I know. You want to keep it. And so you shall. We will have the rest of your ancestress's treasure soon, won't we?" His hands tightened on Susan's shoulders.

Penny had been watching the Silverthornes' reaction, and saw that they were surprised that Susan could wear the necklace. She was pleased and relieved herself, especially to find that Sir Beauford could handle it. That signified that the ghosts had accepted her right to do with it as she would.

She looked at James. His was the only disapproving face. He scowled at the reflection in the mirror of Susan crying, then looked over at Penny. She made herself smile at him, though she had the oddest longing to go and throw herself into his arms, seeking a comforting hug.

"Well! This is wonderful." Sir Beauford turned away from his wife. He had the necklace in his hand. Casually tucking it inside his jacket, he asked, "When shall we retrieve the rest of the treasure?"

"*We* shall not. It would be best that I go alone." Penny gave Sir Beauford a hard look, hoping he would understand the delicacy of convincing the ghosts to give up the treasure directly to him.

"Alone! By no means shall a woman go alone to that castle at night." Thorne's voice was firm. "I thought Lady Winifred told you that you could take James for an escort."

"Ridiculous. It makes more sense for me to go," Sir Beauford suggested. No less than four voices said, "No," with various tones of emphasis. Penny's was the loudest. Sir Beauford shrugged his shoulders.

"Did you ask Jane if she would chaperon you?"
Allison asked.

"Yes. She was a little hesitant, but will go."

"Susan will go with you instead," Sir Beauford
said. "She isn't afraid of ghosts."

"Not at all. I should be fascinated to meet one."
Susan had herself in hand now. "I will go with
you, Penny."

Allison said that she would go, since she could
see the ghosts. Thorne smiled, not entirely pleas-
antly, and suggested they wake up the entire
neighborhood and have a party at the castle.

Allison shook her head at him, her responding
smile not entirely pleasant either. The light of bat-
tle was in her eyes.

Penny did not wish them to come to cuffs over
this matter. She looked at James, who did not dis-
appoint her.

"I shall accompany Penny, as her ghostly ancestress suggested. Susan should do very well for a
chaperon. It is the dark of the moon and the
shorter road is tricky in the dark. We will take the
back route, where there are fewer trees. We'll take
the estate wagon again, since we don't know the
size of this treasure. I'll go tell the butler to have
some hot water bottles and blankets packed in it,
in case we have to wait any length of time. It is
often cold up there at night, even on a warm summer's day."

"Have servants walk in front of you with lights.
Don't hurry, going or coming home," Thorne said.

James nodded and left the room.

Sir Beauford turned his attention to the brandy
bottle again.

"Let me reiterate my previous statement," Thorne

said, placing his hand over the top of the brandy bottle to be sure he had Montrose's attention. "These jewels and other items of property are legally mine. Giving the necklace to Penny made the ghosts quit disturbing my wife's sleep. Her health was in serious danger until then. Nothing leaves my property until I know that the ghosts are satisfied and will leave my wife alone."

Penny spoke up. "I made that plain to Sir Beauford and Susan."

"Indeed she did. And I agree entirely. Wouldn't want a lovely lady such as Lady Silverthorne to be troubled in any way. But at the same time, if Penny has a claim to this property, then my wife, as the oldest, has the better claim."

"Perhaps your mother's genealogy will arrive soon, and we can have a clear picture of the matter," Allison said.

"Genealogy?" Sir Beauford sat up straight in his chair. "What are you talkling about?"

"My mother kept a genealogy of her family. I asked Father to send me a copy of the female line only, as the whole thing is very long. It ends with mother, however. She never added our names to it."

Sir Beauford relaxed. "Susan told me your mother wasn't well in the last years of her life. That would explain it, I expect. Odd for such a plebian family to have kept a geneology through all those years, eh?" He laughed heartily, then subsided when no one joined him.

"Susan, I think we should change clothes," Penny said. "Something a bit heavier, some sturdy shoes, and a shawl or cloak might be better than our evening gowns."

Allison yawned. "I think I will go to bed. It will be a long night. Please wake me when they return?"

Thorne smiled at her. "I will. I hope you *do* go to sleep."

Husband and wife exchanged a glance that meant each knew her ability to do so would tell them a great deal about the truth of Lady Montrose's claims.

The three women absented themselves, leaving Thorne and Sir Beauford to ponder matters. The latter seemed disinclined to small talk, and did not again attempt to pour himself any brandy.

Thorne engaged his guest in a few hands of piquet. But Beauford, whom Thorne knew for a dedicated card player, grew progressively more restive. He declined further libations of brandy and at last threw his cards down.

"I beg your pardon, sir," he said, rising. "Can't seem to keep my mind on the game. Deucedly worried about Susan, don't you know? Think I'll toddle up there and see how things are going."

"Very understandable," Thorne said. "I'll go with you. Show you the way. In this darkness I wouldn't want a guest to mistake the road. We'll ride up."

Beauford went to the French doors, which were open, and stared up at the sky. "No need for that," Sir Beauford said. "I've got eyes like a cat. Can see well enough, I expect. No moon, but lots of stars. I'll go carefully. You go to your lady wife."

Thorne frowned. "I don't think it is a good idea, Sir Beauford. Miss Jones clearly did not wish you to accompany her. Perhaps she feared too many people would frighten the ghosts away."

Sir Beauford shrugged. "In that case, I believe I will go up to my room and lie down a bit. Can't seem to get in the mood for cards."

Chapter Fifteen

*T*horne's eyes narrowed as he watched his guest leave the room. He distrusted Sir Beauford Montrose with every fiber of his being. *Ah, yes. You are going to lie down, while your wife is off on a very odd mission in a potentially dangerous place. You've made a decidedly smoky claim on this treasure, and now you are simply going to rest until your goal is accomplished.* Thorne waited until Sir Beauford had topped the stairs and disappeared from view, then stepped out into the foyer to summon a footman. *I'll have someone keep an eye on that one,* he thought. *My instinct tells me he could be trouble.* He smiled to himself. *We may yet all end up at the castle this night, for if he goes, I will.*

But before Thorne could call out to a footman, he heard a strange sound coming from the corridor that led to Mr. Bartholomew's office and other offices of the hall. It sounded like a woman weeping, loudly. A certain obnoxious woman who had no business being in that place.

The sound drew him to Bartholomew's door. What met his eyes there astounded him. Agatha Kiesley was leaning against Mr. Bartholomew, sobbing for all she was worth, while his worthy long-time secretary held her close and comforted her in a manner that suggested the lover, rather than the kindly friend.

"What is this?"

Agatha whirled around, then nearly swooned into Bartholomew's arms.

"Oh, my darling Edward. I have done this! I have caused you to lose your position. Thorne D'Aumont, you may be Lord Silverthorne now, but you are still the same cruel, careless boy you were when my dear sister—"

"Miss Kiesley. Agatha, dearest. Please allow me to speak to Lord Silverthorne." Bartholomew put her behind him rather more forcefully than she expected, momentarily making her speechless.

"My lord, I can explain."

Thorne crossed his arms. "Pray do. But I should warn you, if that woman once more alludes to my supposed mistreatment of her at the time of my father's and brother's deaths, I shall once and for all expel her from this house. I have taken quite enough of that kind of abuse."

"No, my lord. She will not. Will you, my love?" Bartholomew looked behind him, and apparently received the assurance he sought.

"I take it that you two are in love, then."

"Yes, my lord. I wish to marry her, but of course that is not possible. It would be a mésalliance for her."

"I don't care about that" came a tearful but strident voice from behind him.

Bartholomew's face flushed with pleasure. "At any rate, I am not in any position to support her. I have just now told her of my determination to seek another position, with an eye to someday being able to do so. That is, if she truly wishes to ally herself with a mere servant. I do hope you will consider my years of faithful service and write me a good character."

"You really want to marry this . . ."

Bartholomew drew himself up. His features, often petulant but usually suitably subservient, took on a severity quite unusual for him. "I beg you to remember, my lord, that you speak of the woman I love."

Thorne dropped into a nearby seat. "Well, this is a leveler!"

"I told you he would object because of the class difference. Don't let him convince you, Edward." Agatha came from behind her beloved, ready to fight. "Thorne, your pride is already hurting your cousin, who has the misfortune to love a woman who is beneath him. She knows how you would respond and has made up her mind not to have him, though he, like Edward, would have the courage to face society's strictures if she would only accept him. Now you seek to deprive me of the only chance of happiness I have ever had."

Thorne put his index fingers on either side of his head and massaged his temple. "Good heavens. Do you speak of Miss Jones and James?"

"Of course, you would not notice anything. You are so self-centered. . . ."

"Agatha, my darling, this gains us nothing." Bartholomew again put himself between Agatha and Thorne.

"No, it doesn't," Thorne growled. "And it isn't true. None of it. However, James's and Miss Jones's affairs are not the subject under discussion. Bartholomew, I would like a word alone with you."

"No, no! He will browbeat you. He will turn that look of aristocratic scorn on you and wither all our hopes."

"Agatha, my love . . ."

"Agatha, I stand in the position of your nearest male relative, and as such must negotiate with your fiancé on your behalf, to be quite sure he provides for you."

"My relative! You are no relation to me."

"Then would you explain to me why you are here, in my house, eating my bread and . . . Never mind. Bartholomew?"

"Go to the drawing room, my love." Bartholomew once again assumed a masterful expression. He drew the protesting woman to the door and firmly closed it in her face.

"Barty, are you quite sure that you wish to marry her? She is a harridan, man."

"To you. Not to me. She truly cares for me. We think alike on a great many things."

Yes, you look out at the world with a similar disapproving eye, Thorne thought, though he said nothing.

"I have had no one who cares about my welfare since my mother died when I was ten. I am almost sixty, and tired of my bachelor existence. I know it would not suit you to have a married secretary, sir, for you often need me at odd hours and odd places, not conducive to a married life."

It would not suit me to have Agatha Kiesley living in my home in both country and city forever, either, Thorne thought. He and Allison had been counting the days until the renovations at the dower house were complete, so that he could return Agatha to the home she had occupied once before. He knew that his secretary, by no means a stupid man, realized that. Hence his desire to seek another position.

"Most employers will feel the same," he said.

"I know that, my lord. I have saved a good deal of money over the years, thanks to your generosity. A few more years and I can pay for a small property where I can be a gentleman farmer. Agatha has almost two hundred pounds a year herself. We can live there respectably, if not prosperously, and she won't have the opprobrium of having married a servant."

"A very superior servant, son of a gentleman and himself all that the word implies."

"Thank you for that, my lord." Bartholomew's face reddened with pleasure.

"Agatha is herself somewhat over fifty, though I do not know how much. That means children would be unlikely. So you won't have to provide for that eventuality." Thorne stroked his chin, thinking furiously. "I have a property in Sussex which might suit you, which I could let you have on very favorable terms. A man of your intellect could easily manage it at a profit. I daresay you might do very well there."

Bartholomew stared at him. "You are generous, sir."

Selfish, Thorne thought, mentally rubbing his hands together at the thought of being free of Agatha Kiesley forever.

"I would appreciate it if you would remain in my employ until you have adequately trained your successor. You and Agatha may live in the dower house until then. Once you move, I will lease it, and the revenue shall be hers as my wedding gift to her."

Bartholomew opened and closed his mouth several times before he could stumble out disjointed words of gratitude and apology. "Agatha shall know . . . I shall make her see that you are not . . . my lord, how shall I ever . . . ?"

"By treating her well, man. That is all I ask. As for expecting her to see me in a favorable light, that is so remote a possibility I advise you not to try. I only hope this may make you happy."

"I know that it will, sir, and her, too! Thank you. Thank you!" He wrung Thorne's hand for what seemed like forever before Thorne could propel him out the door.

"Go tell your blushing bride," he said, giving his secretary a final pat on the back that was more of a push.

The sound of renewed weeping accompanied him up the stairs. Thorne could only trust that this time it was a happy sound. *Agatha! Off my hands forever!* He was grinning until he topped the stairs and remembered his mission of a few moments before.

The footman who was always posted nearby seemed to be watching for him.

"My lord, you might be wishful of knowing that Sir Beauford has left by the servants' stairs. He changed into riding clothes and gave me a guinea not to tell you."

The servant held the coin out. Not for a guinea was he going to risk his place with one of the most generous masters in England.

"Keep it," Thorne said. "Send someone to the stables to have a horse saddled for me." He went into his chambers, and slid in though their shared dressing room to check on Allison. She was sleeping, which relieved his mind considerably. Returning to his room, he quickly changed into riding breeches. By this time his valet had arrived and helped him on with his boots. Just as he was slipping into his riding jacket, he heard a sound that struck dread into his heart.

Chapter Sixteen

*T*he group going to the castle had not required servants to light their way after all. Dark as the night was, the sky was so filled with stars that in spots it looked as if a white sheet had been draped over the heavens. James had sent the sleepy men back once he realized he didn't need them, and drove the estate wagon slowly but easily up the long, curving back road to the castle.

As they passed the place where she had encountered the ghost of her ancestress, Penny searched the area carefully, and told the story to Susan.

"I wish I could see her," Susan fretted. "Don't you?"

"Of course. I wish I could talk with her, too, but the last time I did so, it made me faint. No time for that tonight. Besides . . ."

Susan understood the unspoken fear. Penny might order the servant ghosts about, but the ghost of Penny's ancestress might object to her passing the treasure on to Susan, and forbid the other two from bringing the treasure to them. So much was at stake. The two women held hands tightly as they passed the spot.

As James carefully negotiated the narrow neck

of land that led to the castle grounds and was once guarded by a drawbridge and portcullis, a loud honking and hissing sound began.

"What on earth?" Susan asked.

"You've been away from the country too long, love. Those are geese. They've a flock of them that roam the castle enclosure, to warn the watchman that someone is trespassing on the castle grounds."

"To wake him up, is more like it," James said, laughing back at them. "Old Smithfield does more sleeping than watching, I fear. Hoy!" He had to call out three more times to wake up the watchman, by which time the geese had congregated at the gate, honking at the arrivals. Finally a sleepy, tousled-looking man emerged from the gatehouse.

"Oh. 'Tis you, Master James. Ne'er thought I'd have company here on such a dark night."

"Miss Jones's sister, Lady Montrose, is here and wishes to see the place. She's hoping to spot a ghost or two in the dark of the moon."

Smithfield shuddered. "Oh, I hope you don't, ma'am. I ain't never seen one, but the day watchman's wife, Marie, sees 'em all the time, and they upsets her very much."

"Put the geese up, Smithfield. Lady Montrose declares herself more interested than alarmed by ghosts."

They waited in silence as the watchman lured the geese into their pen by shaking a large can of corn back and forth. Then he opened the gate so they could enter. "Was you wanting me to go with you, sir?" His voice had a slight tremor.

"No," James said. "Just keep watch here, eh?" The watchman bowed and tugged his forelock as the wagon passed by him.

"That I'll do, sir."

"He'll likely go straight back to sleep as soon as we're out of sight," James said, laughing.

"Just as well. He might cause problems." Penny sighed.

"Yes, he might object to our taking a fortune in jewels away from here, without Thorne around to indicate his willingness. Mean to say, Thorne and I are best of friends, and I run quite tame here, but that might look a bit suspicious." James stopped the wagon in the center of a wide area of stone pavement. There was no real problem in seeing the buildings and equipment occupying the castle grounds, for they loomed in the starlight as darker shapes than their surroundings. Susan looked with interest at the castle keep.

"Forbidding-looking at night, isn't it?" James asked, holding up his arms to help down first Susan, then Penny.

"Yes," Susan said. "But I should like to explore it by daylight."

"I'm sure Lady Silverthorne will be glad to give you a tour tomorrow." He set Susan down gently, then turned to Penny, looking forward to a brief moment of holding her in his arms.

"Frankly, I'd rather be anywhere else than here," Penny said, shivering as she stepped reluctantly away from James's strong arms.

"I'd find it quite fascinating if . . ." Susan ended on a small sob, at which Penny hugged her.

"It's all right. This is for the best. I only wish I knew what to do now."

"Perhaps you ought to go to that woman beckoning you there." Susan pointed to the north, where fencing blocked off the unsafe areas.

"What does she look like?" James peered into the darkness.

"I can't tell exactly. She is wearing a cloak, with the hood pulled up. She has a sort of glow about her. That must be one of the ghosts." Susan's voice rose in excitement.

"Is she wearing the necklace?"

Susan looked at Penny strangely then. "You don't see her?"

"No. Do you, James?"

James shook his head. "Good thing Lady Montrose can. But don't let her lure you past that fence. I'll stay back a ways." He dimmed the lantern he carried.

"Not far." Penny glanced anxiously up at him. He looked concerned, but without fear. She did not fear the ghost, really. It was the stability of the north wall that concerned her, in spite of Thorne's assurances that it had been made structurally sound. She yearned to lean upon James, or even tarry and let Susan deal with the ghost. But duty forced her to make her feet move, following her sister, who seemed equally as unafraid as James.

"She is looking at you very strangely, Penny. And no, she isn't wearing a necklace. She's wearing an elaborate jeweled hair dress."

"That must be Lady Winifred."

"Is she saying anything?"

"No, she is standing there glaring at you. This doesn't bode well."

"Drat! I need to be able to see her, to talk to her. She must be made to understand. I have an idea." Penny sat down on the ground, her back to a pile of rocks stacked near the fence for the repair of the battlements. "I'll close my eyes. Don't touch me or speak to me for a while." She had no more than closed her eyes than she had that swooning sensation she had known the last time she was in the presence of Lady Winifred. She gave herself over to the strange feelings sweeping through her. Abruptly the darkness behind her closed eyes was replaced by the figure of Lady Winifred.

"What are you about, child? Have we stood watch here so long, just so you can remain in poverty?" The voice was gentle but sad.

"No, Lady Winifred. I won't be poor. I have a position with the Silverthornes that will pay me well."

"Pay! I don't want any more of my children to be poor, to be servants."

Though in one part of her mind Penny knew she was sitting on the ground, she seemed to be standing, facing her ancestress. She lifted her chin.

"I have all that I need. My beloved sister—"

"She is no relation and you know it."

"We were raised together, and I love her as much as any flesh-and-blood sister. Please, ma'am. This is what I want to do with my inheritance."

Lady Winifred threw back her hood. Her blond hair and impressive hair dress made her seem regal, almost queenly.

"You have brought your cavalier. He seems to have great concern for you. He is handsome, rich, and kind. But will he marry a penniless girl?"

"If he won't, I don't want him." It was the first admission she had made, even to herself, that she did want him. "I want him to love me for myself, and not for any fortune I may garner. My sister Susan has just such a marriage, made for personal gain on the part of her husband, and her case is miserable indeed. He beats her and mistreats her."

"So Owain and Bronwyn have told me." Lady Winifred lifted her head and seemed to be looking far away. "I shall permit them to bring the treasure to you on one condition."

"What is that, ma'am?"

"That if this young man offers for you, you will accept. I would have preferred a title for you, but he is an eligible *parti*."

Penny felt a flush on her cheek. Could James hear this? Then she realized it didn't matter, because this time Lady Winifred spoke in Welsh, as her servants had. Penny had sworn never to marry an aristocrat, but she had to promise, for her sister's sake. Deep inside, she knew it would not be a great sacrifice to make.

"If he asks it from his heart, ma'am."

"He will ask." Lady Winifred made an imperious gesture with her hands and suddenly the maid was on one side of her, the soldier on the other. "Bring her the treasure. I then will forgive your trespasses against me. If you can forgive yourselves, you may go on your way."

"And you, my lady?" Penny started to move forward, having again that odd desire to be enfolded in the woman's arms.

"Stay back. I don't wish to steal your warmth and make you ill. I will go to my rest when my bones receive a Christian burial and you have a husband. I want a Catholic priest, mind, not one of your infidel vicars. Until then I will remain on yonder cliff, where I died. Promise me you won't make me wait too long."

"I promise you shall have a Christian burial, ma'am. The other I cannot control."

"Nonsense. All you need to do is give him some encouragement. I can see how he looks at you. He yearns to take you in his arms."

The loud neighing of a horse awoke her from her trance. Penny found herself in James's arms. He sat on the ground beside her, her head and upper body cradled against his chest.

"Thank God. You had us worried." Susan crouched nearby, her hand on Penny's forehead. "You are so cold. Take my shawl."

Over Penny's protest, James took the shawl from Susan and wrapped it around her, over and around her own cloak.

"What happened? One minute you were sitting there quietly. The next you fell over and were flailing and groaning."

Susan laughed lightly. "She was mumbling in Welsh."

"Could you hear and see Lady Winifred?" Penny looked up at Susan.

"No. A short while after you closed your eyes, she disappeared."

"You didn't hear, then?"

"No. But I can guess. She turned you down. Do not worry, sister." But Susan's lower lip trembled.

"She did not. We are to have the treasure, though I don't know where or how or when."

Just then a faint sound, a clink as of metal on stone, caught their attention. The three looked in the direction of the fence. Another, similar sound came, just beyond the wooden palings Thorne had set up to prevent anyone but his skilled workers from approaching the repairs in progress on the battlements.

"No!" Penny turned around and tried to keep James from rising, but he did, bringing her with him.

"I'm just going to open the gate. There is no danger as long as we do not go far inside the enclosure."

Penny's hand clung to his shoulder and slid down his arm as he walked away. Fear gripped her heart. "Be careful."

He turned back and looked at her, and a grin spread across his face. "I will." *She cares for me,* he thought, and felt like jumping straight up in the air instead of calmly opening the gate. When he did, he saw a small pile of objects just inside the door.

"Let me get that lantern and see what we have."

"No," Penny said. "Let's wait until we're sure they've brought all of it up."

"They must have had it nearby," Susan observed as the pile grew rapidly before their eyes. "They couldn't be bringing it up this quickly from any great depth."

How long the three stood watching they didn't know. The time seemed to pass slowly, for none of them felt like speaking, each caught up in wonder at what was happening.

Then Susan drew in her breath sharply.

"What is it?" Penny asked.

"I see two people. The one wearing the ruby necklace is the maid, I suppose. The other is a fierce and blood-covered soldier."

"Are they speaking? Ask them in Welsh if they are finished."

Susan stepped forward a few paces, and addressed the pair. "They both nodded. Now they are bowing to you, Penny." She listened a minute.

"They say you may collect your treasure, and pray your forgiveness for their sin in stealing it."

"Tell them they have it, both from me and from Lady Winifred."

A few more words from Susan in Welsh and silence fell again.

"What is happening?" Penny asked.

"Nothing. They have faded away. I suppose you may collect it now. Quite a pile of it."

"More than I had imagined. I only brought a pillow slip." Penny started toward the wagon.

"I have something better. I brought a large burlap feed bag. An inglorious repository for such a treasure, I know, but needs must!" James chuckled a little as he handed her the lantern and trotted over to the wagon. The horse, which stood with calm resignation where the wagon had stopped, lifted its head and neighed loudly. An answering neigh came from the direction of the gate house.

"That's funny," James remarked as he brought Penny the burlap bag. "I didn't think Smithfield kept a horse up here."

Too interested in the treasure that lay on the ground before her to worry about this, Penny took the burlap bag and hastened to the gate near the pile the ghosts had left. She whistled as she saw what they had brought. Lifting the lantern and inspecting the area carefully to assure herself she would be stepping on solid ground, she moved forward and dropped to her knees. Behind her she heard footsteps.

"It is so much," Susan said in a soft voice beside her. "Push a little aside and keep it for yourself."

Penny was sorely tempted, but she shook her head. "I must keep my bargain so that your husband will keep his," she whispered back. She expected that James stood nearby, as she had heard loud masculine steps as well as the soft tread of her sister.

She filled the burlap bag with an assortment of golden chains, rings, coins, and uncut diamonds and rubies, along with some heavy black chains she guessed to be tarnished silver. It seemed to her to be more than the maid had tossed from the castle window. Then she remembered what the man had said in her first dream, about having confiscated a casket from the maid. *That would explain it,* she thought. Just as she picked up the last item, a ruby ring, she heard Susan gasp.

"Oh, no."

The note of fear in her voice left Penny in little doubt as to what she would find when she turned around. As expected, she saw Sir Montrose standing not far away. She did not expect to see him holding a gun on them.

Hoisting the heavy burlap bag, she marched forward, Susan following behind. "What is the meaning of this. There is no earthly point in it."

"I think you will find that there is. Susan, use his cravat to tie Mr. Betterton's hands behind his back. James, no sudden moves. I have no wish to hurt anyone."

As Susan carried out her husband's orders, James glared at his erstwhile friend. "I am as baffled as your sister-in-law. Why would you take at gunpoint what is already your wife's, or rather, yours, since husbands can control their wives' property?"

"Is he well tied?" Sir Montrose asked.

"Yes. Montrose, please—"

"Please what? I mean no one any harm. It is just that I have pressing debts to pay. I cannot sit around here for God knows how long, waiting for a bunch of ghosts to make up their minds. Sit down, James. Tie his hands to the wagon wheel."

"No!" Penny backed away, into the area inside the gate. "That horse might panic and rock the wagon, hurting Mr. Betterton."

"Still not on first names, Pen? I'd suggest you gather your rosebuds, my dear. Come here."

"I'll throw these things over the castle wall if you hurt Mr. Betterton or Susan." She moved closer to the edge of the gap in the battlements.

"Don't," James called out. "You've gone too far." But she edged farther, holding out the burlap bag in the direction of the abyss.

Susan stood back. "I won't tie him to the wagon."

"Getting brave now, little wifey?" Sir Montrose sneered at her. "Very well, Penny. What would you have me do?"

"Go back to the castle. Keep your agreement to leave the treasure at Thorne Hall for a decent amount of time, to be sure the ghosts don't bother Lady Silverthorne."

Sir Montrose stepped away from James. "Sorry. Some of my debtors are quite out of patience with me. They are the sort that will, at last, take their pound of flesh if payment is not forthcoming. You have had some dealings with such gents, James, old friend."

"I am sorry to be reminded of it. Look, Beau,

we *were* friends and still could be. You've got to do the decent thing, man. I'll loan you what you need until we find out whether Lady Silverthorne is not further bothered by ghosts."

"And what will I pay it back with? I'm at low tide, you see."

"I am sure Lord Silverthorne will pay to keep the treasure, if that is what it takes."

Sir Montrose looked annoyed. "Yes, no doubt he will." He appeared to ponder this a moment. "Very well. Hand the treasure to Susan, Penny."

"After you put down that gun and step away from it."

Montrose reluctantly acquiesced. She stepped forward and placed the heavy sack in her sister's hands, saying as she did so, "I give this to my beloved sister without reservation."

Susan took it reluctantly.

"Why so long-faced, wife? We are rich, after all. Come with me."

"No." She held out the sack to him.

"You will do as I say."

"We have an agreement," Penny said. She had picked up the gun and was kneeling by James, untying his hands as she spoke.

"Extortion. You threaten to expose me to public censure. Well, let me tell you, two can play that game. I can smear you as easily as you smear me. And I'll be believed. Who would believe a penniless little parson's daughter over a member of the *ton*? Did she tell you of our little affair, James? I thought not. Susan wished me to present her to society. It was delicious, having both my pretty little wife and her hot-blooded sister under my roof."

Penny looked into James's eyes, dreading the scorn she would see. What she saw was pure fury aimed at Sir Montrose.

"Now no need to be jealous," Montrose said in a soothing tone, pushing his wife in the direction of the gate. "That affair has long since ended."

"I am quite sure that she ended it rather forcefully, before it began." Finally freed of his bonds, James stood. "You will pay for insulting the woman I love." He launched himself at Montrose, who quickly assumed the stance of a trained boxer, to no avail. Momentum propelled James hard against him, and the two fell to the ground and began to roll over and over, striking at each other as they wrestled. Finally James landed an effective blow and Sir Montrose subsided, groaning in the dark. James stood and jerked the man up.

"Understand me, Beau. You will never speak ill of this woman again. If you do, I will call you to book for it. I doubt you have the stomach for facing a man over pistols or swords. Forcing yourself on women is more your style. Now I have a fair idea of what is going on here, and I will not attempt to stop your taking the treasure once we know that Lady Silverthorne is not tormented by the ghosts. Until then, you will remain here. You will not, however, go near your wife, day or night. You will adhere to that written agreement, or face me. Is that understood?"

He shook Montrose like a rag doll as he spoke.

Swearing, Sir Beauford broke James's hold. "Oh, very well. I don't much care for her anyway. Prim and proper as a parson's daughter." Chuckling over his joke, he reached for the burlap bag full of treasure. He pulled the drawstring tight and knotted the ends. "I'll take that. It would be just like your crazed sister to throw it over the cliff or something. I will meet you back at the house. If Lady Silverthorne sleeps well tonight, I'll be on my way tomorrow. Wife, you may stay with your sister or your father till the end of your life, for all I care. Barren, after all. Barren and boring." He walked off.

Penny drew James into the light of the lantern. "Did he hurt you? I was so frightened when you started rolling about on the ground that you might roll over the cliff or something."

James winced a little as she gently touched his split lip. But then he made it hurt even more by grinning at her. "We were many feet away from that gate. You were the one in the most danger. Going so close to the edge of the castle wall was valiant but foolish. Do you know what, Miss Jones?"

Since he had circled his arms around her so that she couldn't retreat, Penny gave in and did what she really wanted to do, which was move closer. "What?"

"I think you care for me."

"Oh, you do, do you?"

"Yes. And do you know what else?"

"What?"

"I love you. But then, you knew that."

"Oh!" She did not know what to say. The words "I love you, too" sprang up in her heart, but she hadn't quite the courage to utter them. She started to back away, but he tightened his arms.

"I think I deserve a kiss for defending your honor."

"I'd like to point out that we have a witness."

"Good. You'll have to marry me, then." He lowered his head, kissing her cheek since she turned her head away.

"I want no husband because of a 'have to,' sir."

"Foolish beyond permission. Would I be kissing you if I didn't want to marry you? Do you think my affection has altered in this short separation? It didn't. As I traveled to Fairmont, each mile between us made me more miserable. I repeat, I love you. And I want you to want to marry me. Will you?"

She looked up into his eyes. In the dark they had no color at all, so how could they look so warm, so inviting? Why did she feel so warm herself in this high, windy place? Her promise to her ancestress, Lady Winifred, had little to do with the response she wished to make. *I love him,* she admitted to herself.

Penny was just about to accept his proposal when a loud cough distracted them.

Chapter Seventeen

*I*t was a man's cough, but it wasn't Montrose. Smithfield stood next to Susan.

"What is it, man? Can't you see I'm busy?" James snapped. He reluctantly let Penny step out of the circle of his arms.

"Just thought I'd tell you, sir. There was a stranger on the grounds, a man. Had a full burlap bag in his hands. It jangled like it had metal in it."

James scowled at the guard. "It took you long enough to notice."

"Ah. Um, beg your pardon, sir. Fell asleep again, I suppose. Next thing I knew, he was climbing out over the gate, which means he must have climbed in."

"Excellent reasoning." James shook his head at Smithfield, then clapped him on the shoulder. "No harm done. That was Sir Beauford Montrose, this lady's husband."

"So he told me, sir. I did wonder why he didn't wake me, if he had a right to be here. Climbing over the gate! Not what you'd expect from a gentleman. Anyway, thought you might want to know he took the short road. Dangerous, that road, at dark of night under the trees, and so I told him. Told him he should return to the castle by the back road, where there are no trees."

With an irritated sigh, James released Penny. "Yes, it is dangerous. Still, I presume he will go slowly and carefully."

Smithfield cleared his throat again, causing James to pause in the act of helping Lady Montrose into the second seat of the wagon.

"Thing of it is, sir, he ain't goin' back to the castle, I don't think. He asked me for directions to the pike road. That's why he went the way he did. Tried to explain to him about the steep drop-offs and the trees that seem to be right beside the road but are really part of that hanging wood below the road level."

At Smithfield's disclosure that her husband had asked for directions to the pike road, Susan gasped, and Penny put her fist to her mouth. The two women's eyes searched each other's faces for a clue as to their thoughts.

Abruptly Penny began speaking in Welsh. "Oh, Susan. He isn't going to keep the bargain. What if the ghosts aren't satisfied, and take it out on Lady Silverthorne? She is such a good person."

Susan reached out her hands to her sister. "We can't let that happen."

"I don't know what to do. I can't turn my sister back to that man. Yet—"

"You could never live with yourself if any harm comes to your friend. Well, neither could I. And the situation is more dire than you suppose. There won't be any delay in selling those goods. There are men waiting, watching, just beyond the Silverthorne property. They will demand at least a part of the treasure in payment of their debts."

"Worse and worse. Oh, I am so torn."

James stood looking from one woman to the other, surprised and a little annoyed that they were using a language that he couldn't understand.

"You tell him, Penny. All of it. Neither of us can be happy if we cause another woman misery."

Penny sighed. Would this destroy James's trust in her? Indeed, she hardly deserved it, the way she had deceived him and his relatives. He had been about to propose to her. But once he learned how he had been deceived, that proposal might never be forthcoming. And if he did not propose, her bargain with Lady Winifred would be at an end. After all, she had accepted giving the treasure to Susan because she thought Penny would be well-provided for as James's wife. Would the other ghosts return to harass Allison once it became clear that James would not marry her?

In English she said, "James, forgive us for our rudeness in excluding you. There are things you must know."

He waited, eyes holding hers, trust in his face.

"He isn't going back to the castle."

He smiled tenderly and put his hand out to caress her face. "The two of you must think I am a want-wit. Of course, he isn't. My guess is that it would be a bit embarrassing for him now, considering he pulled a gun on me, tried to tie me up, and tried to renege on his word. He'll doubtless find it more congenial to wait for word of Allison's well-being in Buxton. You, Thorne, and I all made it abundantly clear that he was not to sell the treasure until then. He agreed to it. Now we have some unfinished business." He moved to pull Penny back into his arms, but she stepped back.

Susan made a little choking sound and looked to Penny for guidance. "He may not still have the treasure by tomorrow."

James patted her shoulder reassuringly. "One thing about Beau that I do know is that he is too greedy to sell that treasure for a pittance. There is little doubt he will go to London, where he can get the best price."

Both women started to speak at once. James held up his hand for silence. He sought to allay their fears, though he himself was far from easy in his mind. "Anyway, the ghosts let you and Beau handle the necklace, didn't they? That means they accepted your claim to it, Lady Montrose. You are probably unaware of the fact, but anyone else who handled it received such a freezing cold sensation that it made their bones ache. No one could bear to handle it more than a few seconds until Penny came along. That is, until this evening, when you put it about your neck as if it were newly made. As the older sister, I am sure you have made the ghosts very happy by coming to claim your family's treasure. Now would you give Penny and me just a few, few minutes alone?"

"No! James, this is urgent. The ghosts accepted my transfer of the treasure to Susan upon two conditions."

"Conditions? But isn't she the true heir?"

Penny clasped her hands nervously. "No. Susan isn't my sister by blood. I had permission to give the treasure to her. But the conditions haven't been met yet. When the ghosts realize the treasure is gone from the premises, what will their response be? For that matter, we never really tested the proposition that *I* could take the treasure away, much less give it to someone else to take away."

James frowned. "I knew something smoky was going on, but I never suspected that you lied about Susan. You seem so utterly devoted to her."

"I am. I could not care more for her if she were my sister by birth. But she is not. She was adopted by my father at the behest of a nobleman who requested his assistance. I feel so bad about lying!" Penny sobbed and put her head in her hands.

"She was trying to save me," Susan hastened to say in Penny's defense. "He has been a brutal husband. She made him agree to leave me alone if she gave him the treasure. And you know she made him swear he would wait to see if the ghosts would accept his having it and not torment Lady Silverthorne anymore. As you can see, it looks as if he isn't going to keep his word, though."

"I thought he would. I didn't doubt you had enough incriminating information to make him toe the mark." James rubbed his chin thoughtfully. "But tonight, when he showed up with that gun, I should have realized his honor and fear of exposure were outweighed by his desire for a valuable treasure." James knit his brows. "I wish I had not allowed him to leave ahead of us." He slammed his right fist into his left palm. "Foolish Beau! If Allison doesn't sleep well tonight, Thorne will pursue him like all the hounds of hell. He'll never beat him to London to sell his ill-gotten goods."

Susan gave an exasperated huff. "Mr. Betterton, please listen! This is more of a crisis than you seem to realize. He isn't going to London." She explained about the men who, working on behalf of

Sir Beauford's creditors, would waylay him as soon as he left Silverthorne land. "They'll get some, if not all, of what he has."

"Damn and blast. Once they have it, it could be scattered to the four winds in hours." James shouted at Smithfield, "Sound the alarm!"

The guard ran to a tall, slender tower just outside his quarters. Penny knew it housed a bell, for young Jason had begged to have it rung the day they came to the castle for a picnic. His father, though usually so indulgent, had refused, telling him it was only for the purpose of summoning emergency help to the castle. In seconds its loud tolling rang out across the land.

"That will bring help. Wish I had a decent horse." James pondered his options. "I'm going to take the two of you home and then join the chase."

"Be careful, Mr. Betterton. My husband is bad enough, but these men who have pursued him here are vicious. They will kill without mercy."

Penny felt as if she might throw up. She yearned to beg James to stay back, but knew she had no right to ask it, and that even if she had, no honorable man would have stayed behind to let his cousin and such help as he took with him face the danger while he stayed safely at home.

Smithfield had no sooner ceased tolling the bell than they all heard a faint shout, a man's voice crying out. It was followed by the much louder, frantic neighing of horses.

"Come a cropper, 'e did," Smithfield observed, a note of satisfaction in his voice.

"It sounds like it. That could work out for the best, actually. Get a lantern and walk ahead of the wagon. We'll go to him. Ladies, please remain here.

When help arrives, send them down the road to us." He climbed on the wagon, and the two men started down the dark, tree-shrouded road.

Susan and Penny had to do as James said, though Penny chafed at the idea of standing around, doing nothing, while the man she loved walked into the inky blackness toward unknown dangers.

A surprisingly short time later, a number of horsemen came up the treeless back road, moving as quickly as possible in the darkness. They were carrying lanterns, and a wagon rumbled behind them.

The first man to accost the two women was Thorne, who held up his lantern and asked what had happened.

"We don't know for sure, my lord," Susan answered. "My husband took that road in his curricle. It appears he means to break his agreement with us to stay here until we were sure about Lady Silverthorne's well-being. There are some cutthroats waiting for him just beyond your boundaries. If they get their hands on the treasure . . ."

"They mustn't do that until we are sure Allison will be undisturbed," Thorne snapped. "You did well to summon me. But where is James? He can't be trying to pursue him in that farm wagon."

"After Smithfield rang the alarm, we heard a noise. It sounded like a man shouting, and then horses frantically neighing. James took the wagon, and Smithfield led the way, to see what had happened. The horses quit neighing a few minutes before you arrived."

"Sir Beauford must have run off the road in the dark." Thorne motioned his men to follow him. The wagon jostled up and Penny decided she would

not stand for being left in the dark, literally and
figuratively. She waved down the driver.

"We are to ride with you," she said.

The groom seemed puzzled and unsure, but before he could ask any questions or protest, first
Penny and then Susan held out a hand, and he felt
obliged to pull them up on the seat beside him. A
glance into the back revealed to Penny a heap of
blankets, ropes, and pulleys, among other things.

The wagon proceeded at a cautious pace. In seconds they were in darkness so inky that Penny understood why this section of road, overarched by
the thick growth of ancient trees, was so difficult
on a moonless night.

Light from numerous torches ahead guided them
to a place where a sharp drop-off edged the road
on the cliff side. Several men stood around, holding
lanterns up high. Sir Beauford's curricle, much
damaged and with a wheel missing, stood a few
feet away. A groom held and soothed Beauford's
team. James and Thorne stood at the abyss, holding
lanterns and peering over the edge. They were calling out to Sir Beauford, but no answer returned.

They both looked up as the wagon approached,
and Penny was once again struck by how much the
two cousins looked alike. James was three years
younger, and normally it showed, but in the dark,
their worry-furrowed features seemed identical.

James barely glanced at her as he climbed into
the back of the wagon and began tossing off ropes.
She saw that a block and tackle was also among
the gear, and some kind of harness. With the econ-
omy of motion of men who had practiced the ma-
neuver many times, some of the riders rigged the
ropes around a stout tree on the opposite side of

the road. More ropes attached to the block and tackle, and then the harness was held up. James swiftly put it on, shaking his head without looking at her when Penny called out, "No!"

She climbed down from the wagon and hurried over to him. "Why you? Some of these men have been going up and down the sides of this cliff for ages, helping to rebuild the castle."

"I've done it before, too. Thought it quite a lark at the time, but now it will come in handy. It isn't fair to send one of them down. I don't know if Sir Beauford is alive or dead. If alive, I don't know if he'll try to shoot me or welcome me as a rescuer. It's my mess. I should be the one to take the risks."

"How . . . how your mess?"

"For one thing, I knew Beau. I knew he was as tricky as they come. I allowed my feelings for you, my silly amorous mood, to interfere with my judgment, and let him walk away. It is for me to take the risk."

"It's my fault." Susan stepped forward. "I withheld from both my sister and you information that would have allowed you to understand his intentions."

"Do you propose to get in a harness and be lowered down a cliff in the dark of night?"

"I . . ." Susan wrung her hands, and anger filled Penny at the feeling of impotence she knew she shared with her sister at that moment.

Thorne stepped between James and the two women. "The pole lamps are in place."

"Right."

"Be dawn soon," Thorne said, head on one side, a hopeful question in his voice.

"Time might be of the essence."

Thorne clapped him on his shoulder and stepped back, pulling the two women with him.

As if in a nightmare, Penny listened to the calls back and forth as the men lowered James slowly, steering him here or there as he directed, paying out rope as he asked for it. After what seemed like an eternity, he gave a shout. "Here he is."

Silence reigned for another eternity; then James yelled, "Pull."

Every one of the men, including Thorne, took hold of the rope and began pulling. Susan went to her husband's horses. "I'll hold them," she told the groom. "You go help."

The wagon driver had already deserted his wagon, but the horses pulling it seemed content to wait quietly. Penny drew as close to the struggling group of men as she dared.

She took up one of the pole lanterns, which had been laid down by someone now helping pull on the rope. She held it out over the edge and peered into the darkness. First she saw only vague shapes, and then, in the light of her lantern, she could see James, leaning far back and virtually walking up the cliff side. Sir Beauford faced him, draped over him like a large coat. Ropes tied the two men together. Sir Beauford's arms and legs were hanging limply, flapping about as James struggled up the cliff.

James must be exhausted, she thought, and a tremor swept through her that almost made her drop the pole lantern. She forced herself to calm down, and swung the light so that as much of the men as possible was illuminated. In a few more minutes hands reached out and grabbled for James's arms, and then they were on the road.

James's legs buckled, but Thorne was there to hold him up while the men untied Sir Beauford and lowered him to the ground.

Susan ran over and looked down at her husband. She trembled, but her face gave no clue to her emotions.

Thorne and James knelt beside him, listening to his chest, manipulating his limbs, calling his name. There was no response.

James called several of the men to him. He had to be helped to rise. They talked among themselves for a moment, and then to her surprise, one of the other men donned the harness, and several took the rope and lowered him down. He returned in a very short while with something clutched to his chest. It was the burlap bag. With Sir Beauford lying in the roadway, very likely dead, the treasure had been the farthest thing from her mind. Battered and dirty, but intact, it made a metallic clank as the man handed it to James. He walked over to Susan and handed it to her. She let it drop at her feet, apparently as indifferent to it as Penny had become.

James looked disgusted. "He could have saved himself, I think. I found the team struggling to hold the carriage. Properly handled, they could have pulled him free, with only the back wheel lost. I suppose he stood up to whip them forward, but when that thing started to slide off the seat, he let go of the reins to grab for it. They lunged as he had asked for them to do, and over he went. I found that on top of his chest."

Susan began to weep then. Penny went to her and put her arms around her. "Don't, Suze. There was nothing you could do."

"No. No." She shook her head and cried all the more.

"Bring that stretcher," Thorne finally called out. With as much gentleness as possible, the men loaded the unresponsive man onto the wagon. Susan insisted on climbing in and cradling his head in her lap, though it seemed clear that he was not alive. Someone tossed the burlap bag in beside her, but she ignored it.

As all of this had been going on, quite imperceptibly the sky had lightened. Penny only noticed it when the wagon holding her sister started to move. She opened her mouth to protest the danger, then realized that there was enough light, barely, to see the road. She sighed and looked around. Men were mounting up. Thorne helped James into the back of the wagon in which they had ridden from the castle earlier—a lifetime earlier, it seemed. He helped her onto the seat. He then rode alongside the wagon that carried Susan and Sir Beauford. No one spoke.

Chapter Eighteen

A grim procession entered the foyer of Thorne Hall. Four men carried the stretcher holding the lifeless body of Sir Beauford Montrose, followed by his wife, Susan, who leaned heavily on the arm of Lord Silverthorne. Penny followed, her mind numb. James walked just behind her, but he did not offer her his arm. Was it because after his climb down the cliff he had barely enough strength for himself? Or did he now disdain to assist such a treacherous woman?

Several servants stood around, horrified fascination in their eyes. The elderly librarian stood in the door of the library. And in the door of the drawing room, Miss Kiesley and Mr. Bartholomew stood, fixing two equally disapproving glares upon her. She hurried past them, not wanting to hear any of the censure either one or both of them were just waiting to heap upon her. She could not help noticing in passing that Miss Kiesley stood very close to Mr. Bartholomew, and that his hand circled her waist protectively.

Montrose's body was placed upon the bed in his room, and Lord Silverthorne suggested that Susan go to another room to rest for a while.

"No. I must perform a wife's last duty, my lord. No one but me should prepare his body for burial."

Thorne frowned down at the pale, fragile woman. "Very well," he sighed. "I will send someone to assist you, though."

He walked away, leaving Penny standing at the door facing Susan.

"Take this," Susan said, holding out the burlap bag to her.

"No. I gave it to you."

"Under false pretenses."

"To save you."

"I took it under false pretenses." Susan's mouth firmed. "I have no reason to accept it now. I bitterly regret that I ever did. Mr. Betterton said he should have known how tricky Montrose was. Well, I *did* know. Penny, I knew he wouldn't keep his bargain for very long. I just needed a respite. Sooner or later, he would have come for me again. I didn't deserve this gift, and I refuse to accept it."

"Why would he have come for you? You said your father would no longer pay him."

"I could have been an asset to him another way. He threatened me with it if I didn't come here and demand the necklace from you. You see, I have . . . admirers."

"Do you mean he would have taken money . . . ?" Penny couldn't even bring herself to say the words.

"Pandered his own wife. Yes. Disgusting, I know, but it was my problem. I am so ashamed of myself, that I used your love for me the way I have. And now I have probably ruined your friendship with the Silverthornes. You will need that treasure."

"So will you."

She shook her head. "No. Those usurious men will take all of Sir Beauford's assets, of course, including the entailed property, since the entail can be broken now that he has died without issue. But they can't take my family."

"Which includes me. I will take care of you. We'll both go home to Wales. We'll sell this treasure and invest it for the benefit of the whole family."

"No, I meant *my* parents. My father wouldn't be blackmailed by Sir Beauford anymore, but he made it clear that he *will* take care of me. He will recognize me publicly, and provide for me. And whether he does or not, my mother will help me in more subtle ways. So you see, even if the duns take everything, I will not be destitute."

James's deep voice behind them was their first awareness that at least part of this conversation had been overheard. "You let me deal with those cent-per-cent bully boys."

"No!" Both women spoke at once. Penny whirled on him. "You owe us nothing but contempt. And I won't have you risk your life, for they are very bad men."

He searched her face. He had not smiled, or even seemed to be aware of her existence, since the moment he learned she had lied about Susan being her blood sister, true inheritor of the treasure. He didn't smile now, either. He wasn't doing this for her. He was just being kind.

"I won't risk my life," James said. "When news of Sir Beauford's death gets out, the duns will make their claims known. I'll be there, with my solicitor, going over every receipt, making sure it is just and no usury was involved. I shouldn't be surprised if we won't salvage something from Lady Montrose's estate after all." He bowed to Susan.

"And if that is impossible, certainly we can see that no further claims or threats are made against you, Lady Montrose." Thorne's voice told them he had joined them again and had been following the conversation.

Penny felt tears running down her cheeks at the knowledge that these people she had come to care for would do so much for her sister. Penny turned to him slowly, reluctantly. "I owe you an apology, my lord. I have mislead you. . . ."

Thorne shook his head. "It was fairly clear from the first that you were under some sort of coercion."

"I don't feel that justifies my actions. Which makes my request that much more impertinent, but I promised. My ancestress, Lady Winifred, asked me to see that she had a Christian burial. She will guide us to her body, which apparently lodged at the back of an outcropping in the cliff wall opposite the castle and was never found."

"We'll begin searching for her right away."

"She . . . wants a priest. A Catholic priest, that is."

Thorne smiled. "I do not doubt such can be found."

So kind! She did not deserve this, from either man. The burden of guilt became too much for Penny. She ran past her sister, unaware that the bagful of treasure jingled in her hands. When she reached her room, she threw herself onto her bed and gave way to tears—tears of grief and release after the tension of the night before. When it seemed she had shed more tears than her body could hold, she tried to buck herself up by telling herself that at least she could help her family now. She even forced herself to open the burlap bag and look through the myriad items there. Beautiful, ancient, valuable, the treasure was as nothing but dross to her. Nothing could cheer a heart weighed down by the lack of something she had once feared—James Betterton's smiles.

"Susan?" Penny entered the darkened bedroom, in which only one candle burned. Her sister sat by the bed, staring at the body of the man she had married. Tears were streaming down her cheeks.

"Oh, Penny, he looks so handsome lying there. He looks like the man I fell in love with. I wish he had been that man."

"So do I, my darling." Penny hugged her and pulled up a chair next to her. "I do hope that you will forget about going to your father. Why should you expose yourself to further snubs? You can be quite cozy and loved in Wales, whereas in London, among the *ton*, you will be friendless once again, and the subject of gossip."

Susan lifted one shoulder in a shrug. "Gossip will die down. And I won't be friendless. I have made several very good friends, who will feel nothing but relief at knowing I am widowed."

"You have made friends? That short while that I stayed with you, I saw no evidence of acceptance among your *ton* acquaintance."

"It took a while, but I did meet some very good, kind people. And now I will have the Silverthornes when they are in town, and possibly you."

"Me! Not I. I plan to go to Wales and spend my time making my books ready for the printer."

Susan's look of interrogation led her to describe the children's books she had planned to publish. "I doubt the Silverthornes will still want to be involved, but perhaps I can afford to bring one out now. If that sells, I can do more. The work is worthwhile. It will give me great satisfaction to see it to fruition."

Susan smiled. "They are lovely little books. I know they will brighten many children's lives as well as teaching them. I wish I had some such purpose for living. Really, Pen, now that I have grown accustomed to the pleasures of society, I would find it very difficult to bury myself in the parsonage again. No, I expect I will live in society. I may even remarry."

"I am so surprised to hear you say that. My glimpse of the *ton* made me think a woman of our background would live a lonely life there." Abruptly she began to cry. "Foolish creature that I am, I refused a proposal from Mr. Betterton because of that fear. But once I have left this place, I am going to miss him so much!"

"Oh, Pen, never tell me you did so!"

Penny nodded her head.

"The next time he asks, you will not be so silly," Susan said in a very older-sister tone of voice.

"I doubt there will be a next time." Penny slumped in her chair. "If he does propose, I must accept. I gave Lady Winifred my word that I would. But he must now think he has had a lucky escape from such a dishonest person."

Susan leaned over and hugged her. "I don't think so. Wasn't he on the brink of proposing at the castle? If you give him the least encouragement, I believe he will renew his suit."

Penny sighed. "That was before he knew the extent of my lies. And how can I encourage him when I feel so utterly unworthy of his love?"

When Lord Silverthorne entered the room to discuss arrangements for transporting Sir Beauford to his home for burial, Penny slipped away, very low in spirits, and went to the lovely room Allison had given her. She looked around, missing the place, and the friendships she had begun, already.

She was sitting in the middle of the bed, tears trailing down her cheeks, surrounded by the treasure, when a light knock on the door was followed by the entrance of her sister and James Betterton.

"I found this in Montrose's jacket pocket," Susan said, holding out a jumble of rubies.

"The necklace." Penny cried even harder. "Take it. Take all of it away. I can't stand to look at it." She swept the pile of treasure from the bed.

James took the necklace from Susan's hands and walked toward her. "Why are you so upset?"

"I betrayed you and Allison and Thorne. I lied to you. You were all so good to me, and I very nearly placed Allison in jeopardy."

James grinned, and Penny felt her breath catch. He had such beautiful white teeth, such a delicious sideways slant to his mouth. He was smiling at her and coming nearer. She scooted backward on the bed.

"You shouldn't be in my bedroom."

"Your own sister is here to chaperon us." He kept coming. "Do you know what Allison is doing right now?"

She shook her head. The sun was well up, though it was early yet. "Playing with Jason?"

"Sleeping. That's right. She slept like a baby all

night. While you gave the treasure to Beau, while he dashed off to avoid keeping the bargain you made, she slept. She still sleeps, quite peacefully."

"Oh. I am so glad. But that doesn't change what I did."

"You are too hard on yourself." He laid the necklace down on the end of the bed and reached into his vest, pulling out a folded, sealed piece of paper. She recognized it as the document she had given him some hours earlier.

He began to open it.

"I didn't give you permission . . ."

"I swore to you I would not open it unless you or Lady Montrose were in danger. . . ."

"That's not how I worded it. And the danger is past, at any rate."

He sat on the bed next to her. "I have decided you are in danger of throwing away two friends and one lover who would be your husband if you could forgive yourself for what you did. Therefore, I deduce I have the right to read it."

Lover! Husband! She caught her breath at the thrill of hope lancing through her. She glanced at Susan, who nodded her head.

"Very well."

He opened the document and read Montrose's confession of the way in which he had tricked his wife into marrying him, the way he had blackmailed her father, and the way he had abused her. His practice of cheating at cards was detailed, too.

"And finally, you had him write in his own hand that he would not leave the premises of Lord Silverthorne until it was quite certain that Lady Silverthorne would not be disturbed by the ghosts. He further agreed to keep the treasure for some time after he left here, and to sell it only to reputable dealers with a buy-back agreement in the event the ghosts began to object once he left here in possession of the treasure.

"Now." He folded the paper back up. "I may be prejudiced, but I think that shows a great deal of concern for Allison. I intend to show this to Allison and Thorne, not that I think them in the least disposed to object to your attempts to save your sister from an odious husband. Such a document is proof that you did not put Lady Montrose's well-being above Allison's, isn't it?"

"I . . . but we have seen how inadequate my measures were."

"It is the intention that you should judge yourself on. Certainly it is what I judge you on."

"You . . . you looked so . . . hurt, and, oh, I don't know, disinterested when you learned I had lied. You wouldn't look at me, or smile at me." Penny certainly took note of the fact that James had sat on the bed beside her, but she didn't do what a proper young woman would. She didn't object. Instead, she found herself leaning toward him.

"I suppose I was hurt a little, that you didn't trust me enough to confide in me. But mainly I was shocked because I realized just how terrible Beau must have been to his wife, to make you risk so much, give so much up, for Susan, when she wasn't even your blood relation. And I also realized that your rejection of me may have been based on his behavior. Very lowering thought, that."

"Oh, James. Is that true?"

"Yes. But really, Penny, you don't think I would behave as Sir Beauford did, do you?" He looked at her anxiously.

She shook her head. "No. Not now. I know you are a good man." She felt his hands grasp her, and somehow found herself sitting in his lap, which meant she must, perforce, put her arms around his neck to keep herself from sliding off. That led to something else, something Penny had never known to be a pleasant experience. His lips came down upon hers with great tenderness, and it was she who pressed back, intensifying the kiss. A hungry growl in James's throat reassured her that this was highly acceptable to him.

Several minutes later she came to her senses and pulled away. "What will Susan think?" She looked around. Her sister had gone.

"I hope our happy marriage will help her know she need not fear loving again, someday."

Penny leaned against him, a little frown on her face. "Oh, James, are you sure? Your friends will look down on me, you know. The *ton* will treat me as an interloper."

"My true friends will not. You are judging them before knowing them. Besides, you are now a wealthy heiress with royal blood. I doubt not that you will become society's darling. Were I not so wealthy myself, they'd accuse me of being a fortune hunter." He smiled down at her, and she noticed again how very long his eyelashes were. This close, she could even see some golden flecks in those deep brown eyes.

"Royal blood? We can't prove that, though Lady Winifred said it was so."

"Oh, I suspect we can. Old Swinton has found some interesting documents that can directly tie your ancestress to Charles I. He just cornered me in the morning room and told me all about it."

"Really?" Penny leaned back against him. "I care nothing for such things. My father would say it is one's own character that is important, not one's bloodline."

"I agree entirely."

"Still, I suppose it will help in society."

"Kiss me again, and let society go hang."

So she did.

Her father's tiny church in Brecon, Wales, had never been so full. For the wedding breakfast afterward, they had been forced to set up tables outside. It was a fair bet that the residents of Brecon had never seen so many titled people in their town.

Her father officiated with tears in his eyes. Lord Silverthorne gave Penny away, so her father wouldn't have to do double duty. Susan stood beside her, looking much younger than that night a year ago when she had arrived at Thorne Hall. Observing her tenderly was Lord Martinvale, who had recently claimed her as his daughter. In the seat just behind him sat Lady Hartnet. When she was so near to Susan, the resemblance between them was striking. *So that is why Lady Hartnet was so very good to me,* Penny thought, glad to have Susan's parentage traced to two such decent people.

Penny wore a white satin robe, very *à la mode*, and a quite unusual decoration to go with it, a ruby necklace of elaborate, old-fashioned design. It was far from a fashionable wedding bauble, but everyone there knew its significance, and felt that it was just exactly what she should wear.

There were other attendants at the wedding, though as they stood at the altar Penny and her beloved James did not see them. Little Lord Riggswheel pointed to the ceiling of the church and started to call out.

"Not now, sweetheart," Allison whispered in his ears.

"But it is the lady. And the maid. And a fierce-looking—"

"I know. They've come to see our dear Penny married. Wave to them, but don't speak now. This is a time to be quiet."

So, wide-eyed but unafraid, the little boy waved to the unseen guests, who solemnly bowed to him in return, before fading from sight.